Skye, Revised

by

Pamela Spradlin Mahajan

Skye, Revised

Contact Information: info@thewildrosepress.com

Cover Art by *The Wild Rose Press, Inc.*

The Wild Rose Press, Inc.
PO Box 708
Adams Basin, NY 14410-0708
Visit us at www.thewildrosepress.com

Publishing History
First Edition, 2024
Trade Paperback ISBN 978-1-5092-5400-2
Digital ISBN 978-1-5092-5401-9

Published in the United States of America

Dedication

For my mom and alpha reader, Gail. Thank you for showing us that anything is possible.

Chapter One

Skye

"Really? You're going to wear that?" I said.

Teddy gave his outfit a once-over. "Yes…" The corner of his mouth inched up into a smile. "Is there something wrong with it?"

I wrinkled my nose as if a reeking can of fly-ridden garbage sat rotting nearby. "Khakis, Teddy? Pleated khakis?" I hadn't even mentioned the cheap tucked-in polo shirt. "It looks like the uniform you wear on the show."

Teddy swiped his jacket from the coat rack by the door and slipped into it. When it was sixty-one degrees in Los Angeles, you wore a jacket. "And, again, I ask: what's wrong with that? Come on, Skye. We're gonna be late."

I exhaled an exasperated gush of air.

"You look great, by the way. The black really makes your blonde hair stand out." Teddy lifted my knee-length coat from the rack and slid it over my form-fitting dress. I glanced down at the sheer cutout stretching across my collarbone.

"Well, it's a nice place. I want to make a good impression—to look like we belong there."

Teddy's outfit did not demonstrate that we belonged anywhere worth being—especially not somewhere like The Hibiscus. It attracted A-list, red carpet fixtures the way spandex boy-cut underwear attracted wedgies. I was quite certain pleated khakis would be nowhere in sight, unless they were being worn ironically.

I side-eyed his chain-store-salesman look once more. It never failed—no matter how many slim, trendy trousers or jeans I picked out for him from Banana Republic or Asos, he still reached for the very same familiar item in the bowels of his closet. The very one I was trying to direct him away from. Honestly, what was the point?

My body ached with the exhaustion of defeat as I slid into the passenger seat of Teddy's hatchback.

"Are you excited? You've been wanting to go here for years," he said as he maneuvered out of the parking lot.

I'd be more excited if your outfit didn't embarrass me.

I mumbled a nondescript response and we sat in silence for several minutes. As we pulled onto the 101, Teddy grasped the leather-wrapped steering wheel with one hand and rested the other on my bare knee. I glanced at his hand, watching the tendons move beneath his tan skin.

Then I gazed out the window as decrepit buildings morphed into sleek, glossy high-rise apartment complexes. Los Angeles was forever an unsettling contrast between seedy and superior, sad and spoiled. The only consistent thing was its palm trees. As I studied a tree outlined against the sky, my stomach knotted into a mixture of excitement and dread.

We had never been to The Hibiscus before—we'd

never been anywhere close. Teddy considered Red Lobster a classy establishment, for God's sake. In my opinion, anywhere you have to wear a bib while eating is definite no no.

I took a measured inhale. The thought of Teddy's stale outfit being scrutinized by L.A.'s hippest wasn't the only reason for my frazzled nerves. I was replaying a conversation between us from several days earlier, searching it for hidden meaning. For clues.

"Ketan proposed to his girlfriend last week," Teddy had said about his brother as we brushed our teeth over the small pedestal sink in his bathroom.

"Oh? That's great..."

"Yeah. He did it at a minor league baseball game. Had it all set up so they were on the Kiss Cam. Then he just got down on one knee—"

"Aw, that's cute." I bent forward to spit, holding my oversized sleep shirt out of the crossfire.

Teddy dropped the toothbrush from his mouth, letting it hover over the sink. "He said the audience cheered for them. Would you like something like that? Something so...I don't know... public?"

I swallowed, my neck stiff as I stared directly ahead. "What does it matter what I would want? It's cute for them, though." I placed my toothbrush in the ceramic cup, then rinsed out my mouth with water.

"But what would you like?"

I inhaled sharply before turning to Teddy. His brown eyes were sincere as they searched mine.

"I don't like baseball. So...probably not that."

Teddy finished brushing his teeth, spit, and returned his toothbrush to the container. "Good to know," he said, smiling slightly.

And that had been the end of it.

Now as I glanced sideways at him in the car, I scanned his body for any sign of nerves or trepidation. What was this swanky reservation about? Was Teddy planning something? Was he going to propose tonight? A cold metal claw clamped around my heart at the thought.

With my head spinning through the remainder of the drive, we seemed to arrive at the restaurant fairly quickly, especially considering L.A. traffic. Teddy and I were soon trailing a hostess with perfectly drawn-on eyebrows and a lithe figure through The Hibiscus. The eatery was known for its hidden alcoves, which were perfect for famous people seeking privacy.

As we walked, I wondered anxiously where we would be seated—and who would we be seated next to. Did Teddy request a special table? But as we passed rows of high-backed booths and navigated around private areas surrounded with overflowing ivy boxes, I went cold and clammy. It was as if the hostess was leading us right out the back door. Was this some kind of a cruel joke?

"Here you are." The hostess dropped our menus on the table. "Enjoy."

I couldn't catch my breath for a few seconds. We had stopped at a small bistro table situated against the tiny slab of wall between the men's and women's restrooms. Why was there even a table here? My cheeks burned hot. I wanted to fall to my knees and crawl away. This was utterly humiliating.

Teddy's face reddened. He reached over and stroked my arm.

"I'll talk to them. See what I can do." He

disappeared from view.

I lingered beside my chair, not wanting to sit. Was this actually going to be my first—possibly my only—dining experience at The Hibiscus? Sitting toilet adjacent? What if someone saw me here? What if my coworkers or, *God forbid,* my boss saw me dining steps away from where people were splashing urine all over the walls?

Teddy reappeared, his face redder now and decidedly more solemn.

"I'm sorry, Skye." He spoke as if he was telling me my best friend had died. "They said there's nothing they can do. Apparently, they have a big celebrity dining here tonight. They didn't say *who.*"

I narrowed my eyes at him. "They've always got a big celebrity dining here. That's most of their clientele."

Teddy shrugged, pulling out my chair. "Well, anyway—can we make the most of it?" His voice was gentle as he held out his hand toward the chair, urging me to sit.

I gritted my teeth and plopped down, a surge of anger shooting through me. How could he be so ineffectual? Had he even really tried to get us a new table? I knew I should have talked to the hostess myself.

"Did you offer her money?" I said, scooting up to the table.

"I don't have that much cash on me." Teddy sat down. "It's more about *who* you're dining with than *where* you're dining anyway, right?"

I glared at him, silent. Teddy's face fell. He appeared wounded.

"Listen, I'm sorry it's not up to your standards. I tried to—I wanted to make it special. I really tried everything I could." Teddy adjusted his spoon and knife, then mussed up his thick blond hair. "I'm sorry you're disappointed. That's not what I wanted."

I stared down at my menu. What *I* wanted was to get out of the seat and The Hibiscus as fast as my shaky legs could carry me.

"Should we just have appetizers?" I said.

Teddy scrunched his eyebrows together. "Are you kidding? It took months to get in here. I don't know about you, but I'm having a real meal. Isn't the food what they're known for?"

A slim, young waiter outfitted in the restaurant's crisp black-and-white uniform appeared. "Good evening. Can I start you off with some wine?"

"Yes, absolutely." Teddy fumbled with his menu.

"Here is the wine list, sir," the waiter said, sliding it out from beneath Teddy's menu.

"Oh, thanks…um, what's on tap?"

"It's wine," I said, my face hot. "There's no wine on tap." I glanced sheepishly up at the waiter. "Could you just give us each a house Cab, please?"

"Certainly."

"How was work today?" Teddy asked once the waiter had disappeared.

I struggled to focus my thoughts. "Okay. Francesca's on the warpath since we've taken on Sissy Stone as our newest PR client. She wants everything to be perfect, of course."

Teddy's phone buzzed. He slid it out of his pocket and stared at it.

"It's Caroline. She's asking if we can meet this

weekend to go over next week's wardrobe." He put the phone away. "Sorry. I put it on silent."

My top lip curled as I pictured Teddy's pretentious producer, Caroline. Of course *she* would be angling for more time with him. She was so clearly into him.

Teddy slid his hand across the table and interlaced his fingers with mine. "Can we just try to have a good time? Salvage the evening?"

I stared at our interlaced fingers as Teddy massaged the crook of my hand with his thumb. "Sure," I said, forcing a smile.

We ordered soon after and sipped our wine as we waited for our food. When our artisan dishes were finally presented—his was a neat little filet mignon topped with a sprig of mint leaves and mine was a fresh Icelandic Salmon—Teddy put his hands in the air.

"I won't touch anything until you take a picture," he said.

Teddy respecting my habit of documenting fancy meals on my Instagram was sweet. I hadn't considered doing it that night, and yet—the top of the table would give no indication as to *where* we were seated. Our meals did look particularly photo-worthy. If someone happened to ask me where we had been seated, I would just—*lie, lie, lie.*

I held my phone over the table, rising from my seat a few inches to achieve the perfect angle. After snapping several shots, I sat down and glanced at Teddy. Smiling, he gave me a wink.

"Shall we?" he asked, gesturing toward our plates.

I nodded.

"You know, there's a reason I asked you here tonight, Peters."

I didn't dare look up. I just stared intently at the glazed salmon on my plate, waiting for him to elaborate while hoping he would drop the whole thing. I struggled to swallow.

I attempted not responding, but couldn't help blurting out, "Being thirty Teddy, I'm sure you're ready to—"

A high-pitched squeal made us both turn. I looked once, then twice to be sure I was really seeing what—and who—I thought I was seeing. A bleached-blonde woman with a comic-book tiny waist and a big rear end hustled toward us…or rather toward the bathrooms beside us. A small girl of about eight trailed her, gazing up like an adoring Spaniel.

"You're my idol," the girl said, sipping in gulps of air as if she might hyperventilate. "I want to be just like you. I loved you on *Countdown to Famous*!"

Sissy Stone paused and grimaced, glancing left and right. Then she snatched the pad and pen from the girl's grip.

"Thanks," Sissy mumbled, her lips pursed. After scribbling something down, she shoved the pad back at the girl and disappeared into the restroom.

"Oh my gosh, oh my gosh, oh my gosh!" the girl squealed before running back into the restaurant.

I couldn't help but ponder how that child had gotten a better table than us. Her mommy or daddy must be somebody important. As I considered this, a forty-something man rushed forward, his index finger pressing on what appeared to be an earpiece. He paused beside our table, standing at attention as he stared in the direction of the women's bathroom.

"She just entered the ladies' restroom. Over," he

said.

Once upon a time, Sissy Stone and I had been equals. Two years ago, we had both waited five-plus hours at the same audition for the second season of the star-making singing reality show, *Countdown to Famous*. While Sissy Stone had been plucked from obscurity and gone on to sing at the Academy Awards, win multiple prestigious Sonny Music Awards, and bed some of the hottest male stars alive, Skye Peters (aka me) had been mocked by one of their foul-mouthed judges and ceased to ever sing again. But I wasn't bitter. Not. At. All.

"You want to go say 'hi' to her? Since she's your newest client?" Teddy asked, taking a bite of his steak.

"She's not *my* client, Teddy. That's not how it works."

"Well, it's all worth it though, huh? We got to see a celebrity."

I paused, my eyes bulging. "Seeing celebrities is part of my job. Why would that be a bonus?"

Before Teddy could respond, a loud, jarring noise made us both turn once again. A man in low-slung jeans that were weighted down with chains sprinted toward the women's bathroom. The bodyguard promptly stuck out his arm, clothes-lining the rabid fan just before he breached the bathroom's threshold. The man dropped hard to the floor. But the rapid fan wasn't going down without a fight.

As the bodyguard got onto his knees to apprehend him, the man swung his fists wildly. The guard fell backwards onto my elbow, knocking the glass of Cabernet I was holding directly into my face. Teddy jumped from his seat and came over to place himself between me and the scuffle. But the guard quickly gained control of the situation and escorted the man away without so much as an "Excuse me." Sissy exited the bathroom minutes later and strutted back into the restaurant, none the wiser.

"This night is officially a disaster." I snorted, attempting to expel the wine that had gone up my nose.

Teddy handed me a napkin, and I dotted my wine-soaked skin. "It was kind of exciting, though. Maybe it will make the evening news. Maybe we'll be famous."

I looked up, eyes narrowed and jaw clenched. "Seriously? You think this is exciting? I want to get the hell out of here *now*."

Teddy took a step back as if I had pushed him. "You haven't eaten your salmon."

"I'll take it to go." I crossed my arms and stared pointedly at a plant nearby until Teddy wandered back to his seat. He plopped down and gazed listlessly at his half-eaten meal.

"I'm sorry—"

"Stop apologizing. It doesn't make anything better."

When the waiter came by to check on us, Teddy requested two to-go boxes and the check. Then he cleared his throat.

"What I wanted to say earlier was…" He reached into his pocket. Surely, he wouldn't think of proposing—not after all of this.

I watched as Teddy fished something out of his khaki pocket. Finally, he dropped a folded piece of paper onto the table. "I booked us a room at a B&B for the weekend."

"Oh."

"But I'll probably just disappoint you then, too."

I didn't have the energy to deny it. I tended to agree with him.

"Here you go, folks. Have a great evening." Thc waiter placed two plastic boxes on the table.

But that ship had sailed long, long ago.

"Here, I'll get yours." Teddy reached across the table and used his fork to slide my salmon into one of the plastic boxes, then boxed up his filet mignon.

"Thanks." I inhaled. "Listen, Teddy. Sorry if I've been harsh. I've just been looking forward to this for so long."

Teddy looked up at me through his eyelashes, flashing a weak smile that didn't reach his eyes.

"I know."

As we walked back through the restaurant, I spotted the autograph-seeking girl in one of the ultra-private booths beside the wafting jazz of a live band. She was sipping a colorful, umbrella-accented drink as a solicitous waiter refilled her smug parents' wine glasses. The girl's cheeks were pink with joy.

My heart fell at the sight of them. Was I the butt of some cosmic joke? When would I be the one with the prime dining spot—the one overflowing with unabashed joy?

Chapter Two

Skye

"She's coming *to*-day."

I looked up from my phone to Francesca's frantic face. My boss was standing at the front of the room, just outside her glass-encased office. Dallas and Denver were at their desks on either side of me.

"Yes, we know." Denver's tone was bored as she ran a file against the top of her nail. "And we're doing all we can..."

"Did you literally just say that to me—" Francesca said. "—when you're *filing your nails?*"

Dallas scooted out from behind her desk, hurried toward Francesca, and put a red-tipped hand on each of her shoulders.

"Remember, you always get like this before we meet a new client." Dallas spoke as if she were calming an irate child. "But we've got everything under control. We've been planning this for weeks."

Though Dallas and Denver were not sisters, they looked as if they could have been. Both women were tall and willowy, with long blonde hair and skinny limbs that flitted around from texting to typing to delivering Francesca her morning latte. Incidentally, they were also both named after the cities they were conceived in.

"It's just so *unromantic*," Denver had complained of her name shortly after we met. "Why not just name me Philly or Tucson?"

I looked up as Dallas continued moving her hands over Francesca's shoulders in a sweeping motion. It seemed to be working. Then, the shrill ring of the phone jolted Francesca back to a frantic state.

"I got it," I said, raising my hand authoritatively.

"Hello," said a male voice on the other end. "This is Roger, Personal Assistant of Sissy Stone."

"Yes, hello?" Though I felt tense, I gave Francesca a confident smile.

"I need to go over what will happen today during Sissy's powwow with Francesca. Who am I speaking to, please?"

"Oh, um, Skye Peters, Associate Public Relations Professional."

"Is Francesca available?"

Noting my boss's bloodshot eyes, I decided to protect her from further stress. "She's…indisposed. I can assist you."

Sighing with a mixture of irritation and ambivalence, Roger went on. "Okay, will there be a private room where Sissy can freshen up?"

"Um…" I glanced around the open-style design. It consisted of three metal desks positioned outside of Francesca's office. My eyes darted to the conference room. "Sure, yes, of course."

"Terrific," Roger said blandly. "Sissy likes every room she enters to be filled with a large, let me repeat, *large* vase of crimson red—that's crimson red, not pink, not yellow, and *not* pale red—roses. And she likes the room to smell like roses. So, a floral-scented candle may be necessary."

I swallowed, scribbling down his comments. *Roses. Deep Red. Scent everywhere.* I underlined "everywhere" as Francesca, Dallas, and Denver stared at me in tense silence. "Okay, sure, terrific."

"And Sissy asks that no one make eye contact unless she makes eye contact with them first and says the magic word."

Roger paused, making me fear I was supposed to know what the word was. Luckily, he proceeded.

"Well, then."

Though that was technically two words, I held my tongue.

"We'll make sure everything is set up to Sissy's specific needs. She has nothing to worry about. We'll see her soon."

"Uh-uh." *Click.*

"I literally could not breathe the whole time you were on the phone," Francesca said the moment I returned the phone to the desk.

"Okay, why?" I asked, not pausing for a reply. "It's fine. We just need to get some gorgeous red roses—a lot of them, in deep red—and some rose-scented candles. Also, no eye contact unless Sissy says—"

"Well, then," Denver interrupted.

"Uh, yes—" I stared down at my notes. "So I'll head to the florist right now and—"

"Dallas, get on that," Francesca said, not looking at me.

Dallas nodded before power-walking to her desk, grabbing her purse, and bursting out of the door.

"Denver, head to the local shops and find the chicest, most delicious-smelling rose candles you can sniff out. Buy twenty of them."

Denver got up slowly and meandered out of the office without looking up from her smartphone. My body slowly filled with cortisol as I sat dumbly at my desk.

"Skye," Francesca went on, her microbladed brows raised severely. She pulled a slip of paper from her pocket, marched over to me, and held the paper inches from my face. "I need you to refill my anti-anxiety medication. *Pronto.*"

I took the paper she was wagging in my face. Francesca spun on her heel and hurried away, mumbling, "And I have to call the caterer, and make sure there's enough Kombucha…"

So I was good enough to pick up her medication, but not good enough to secure last minute items for Sissy Stone? It seemed as if she'd always preferred the Uber-Model Twins over me. Dallas and Denver both grew up in L.A., while I had grown up in the sticks of Northern California. They could afford Gucci and Stella and Prada without a second thought, while I had to lurk around Poshmark like it was my second job. Dallas even had a brief but successful stint as a pop singer when she was a teenager, once winning an MTV Music Award.

Feeling dark and bitter, I rose from my chair, grabbed my fourth-hand Chloe bag, and stalked out of the office. I kept my phone in my lap on the short drive to the pharmacy, my eyes darting downward at every stoplight or pause in traffic. Trepidatiously, I opened the Instagram app and waited. Since last night, the photo I had posted of our meal at The Hibiscus had garnered…eleven likes? Seriously?

My cheeks burned as I mindlessly clicked on Dallas's name (she was one of the people who had liked my photo), and reviewed her latest image. It showed her in a pale pink sports bra and skin-tight leggings, squatting beneath a weight she held behind her neck. The photo was actually of a mirror image of all this, no doubt taken by Dallas's personal trainer.

My eyes dropped below the image—three-hundred-seventy-five likes. Before I could fully react, a blaring horn jolted me back to the present scene: my car, in the middle of Wilshire Boulevard. I had neglected to notice that the person in front of me had accelerated. I jammed my foot down on the gas pedal.

Who knew the true meaning of the numbers—if there was any meaning at all—but, to me, that eleven said: You're just a backwoods girl who will never measure up. Even if the likes were just bots, Dallas still knew more about how to play the game than I did.

I had once dreamed of becoming a famous singer. But even thinking the words "my singing" now filled me with a dump-truck-load of shame. *Your singing? What singing?* I had not sung in years, not even within the private confines of my own apartment.

When I was back at the office, Denver responded to my complaints about the forced medication run by dropping a massive stack of magazines atop my desk. They landed with a loud *thud.*

"Here," she said. "You want to do something related to Sissy? You got it."

I gaped at the magazines, which towered over my head.

"Go through each one of these gossip rags, page by page, and make a note whenever you see Sissy. Open up the 'Sissy Press' doc in our shared drive and fill out the answers to all the questions."

"What questions?"

Denver began listing things off on her long, slender fingers. "If the press is generally favorable or unfavorable, if she's alone or with someone. Who that someone is, if she's showing cleavage, legs, ass or all three…you get the picture."

As Denver breezed back to her desk, I pulled a magazine out of the stack and laid it open in front of me. A few pages in, I scored my first Sissy sighting. It was in a section labeled "Star Shots" which appeared to show celebrities doing average, everyday things like walking their dogs, getting coffee, or sauntering down the street with shopping bags in tow.

In this particular shot, Sissy wore a knit crop top and booty shorts that revealed her overflowing curves. Her hair was dyed bright pink and pulled into spiky pigtails. She looked solemn as her eyes darted sideways.

I began typing all this in the document, then I studied her companion. The man was tall and well-built with nicely groomed dark hair and eyes. *Damn.* He was hot. As I stared, I noted that the man's broad shoulders practically burst out of his knit henley, and his impressive hands, which hung at his sides, were quite large. He appeared older than Sissy, maybe in his mid-forties. I lowered my head, reading the caption.

"Pop tart and *Countdown to Famous* winner Sissy Stone is seen leaving celebrity favorite Louie's Diner with very married record producer Mark Campbell after a late-night chow fest. Illicit waffles with a side of guilty grits, anyone?"

"Hey, Denver. Is Sissy dating some married producer named—" I stared down at the caption again. "—Mark Campbell?"

"Girl, what rock have you been living under?"

"I'll take that as a yes."

I googled his name. The second video that came up was of him on the red carpet. Next to him was a petite brunette woman who looked—*gasp*—about his age. I pushed play.

"This is my beautiful wife, JoJo Stern." Mark held out his arm to present her. Lights flashed around them, and attractive people dressed in evening wear milled about.

Mark had what sounded like a Scottish accent, which only served to increase his sex appeal. This made me think of Teddy's accent in comparison, which consisted of a slight Minnesota twang.

I studied JoJo. She was short and curvy with the body of a former cheerleader. After Mark introduced her, she turned in a slow circle to show off her floor-length sparkly gown.

"Where are the kids tonight?" the off-screen reporter asked.

"They're at home, probably watching right now." JoJo's face lit up. She looked directly at the camera and waved. "Hi, Lucienne. Hi, Comet. Finish your homework!"

I kept scrolling until I came to a video with Sissy's name in the title. It looked as if it was taken on the same walk out of Louie's Diner as the earlier tabloid photo. I scrolled back to the first video with Mark's wife to check the date: late last year. Then, back to the current video: a few months ago. I pushed play on the

Mark and Sissy video.

"Where's JoJo, Mark?" a man shouted from off-camera.

Mark and Sissy maintained a large distance between them, most likely to avoid being photographed together. But why go to a popular diner if you didn't want to be photographed?

I studied both of them as the video progressed. Mark was serious and silent, but he seemed composed. Sissy, on the other hand, appeared visibly upset. Eventually, she pulled a hoodie over her pink pigtails and sunk into herself.

"Are you a homewrecker, Sissy?" said a man as he rushed her and held a camera overhead.

I couldn't be sure, but I thought I saw her flinch. Mark didn't react. He just continued walking, seemingly unperturbed.

The buzzing of my phone interrupted my engrossed state. I slid over and checked the screen. It was a reminder of my lunch with Maxie. I smiled, leaning over to lock my computer.

"Heading out to lunch," I said, lifting my bag and heading toward the door. "See ya later."

"Quickie with Ted?" Denver called out.

"*Denver,*" Dallas reprimanded, disgust evident in her voice.

I rolled my eyes and continued out the door without comment.

****

Maxie and I sat at Ringo's, a cute little bistro in Brentwood, at a sun-drenched patio table along the sidewalk. Maxie lived thirty minutes away in one direction and I worked twenty minutes in the other, so we often met here for lunch.

As the palm trees beside us rustled gently in the breeze, Aston Martins, Ferraris, and Lamborghinis sped by on the street. Two tables over, a pair of glossy-haired blondes with expensive highlights shared their table with two designer bags worth thousands of dollars each. Opulent wealth was always on display in L.A. I used to believe I would one day possess it as well—that I would be One of Them. That belief slipped away more and more each day.

"I'm Francesca's glorified personal assistant," I said. "I'm supposed to fetch her dry cleaning, take her car to get it detailed, and pick up her prescriptions from the pharmacy. That's not my title. That's *not* what I was hired for."

Maxie lifted her fruity alcohol concoction and sipped. In the bright L.A. sunshine, a striking auburn tint danced across her neat afro. Her strapless purple sundress showed off the luminous cocoa skin at her collarbone and shoulders.

"Why do you stay?" she asked, swallowing a sip of the frozen drink.

I picked tentatively at the potato salad sitting next to my veggie burger and sweet potato fries. "Paying my dues? I think?"

"Well, let's change the subject to something happier. Say, your weekend getaway with Teddy-boy?" She paused. "Dang, girl. You've stared at your phone every five seconds since we sat down. Expecting a call?"

I glanced up from the phone lying between us on the metal tabletop.

"Only eleven likes on my latest Insta post. It's

pathetic."

Maxie picked up her chicken wrap and took a bite. Then, she dotted the sides of her mouth thoughtfully. "Why do you even care? It's not like it means *anything.*"

"No idea. But I do care. I can't help it."

"Do you think Teddy's going to propose this weekend?"

I dropped my fork. "Seriously? Don't even joke about that. Ugh." My appetite had abruptly vanished.

Maxie tilted her head, wrinkled her brow, and puffed out her lips sympathetically. "Would it really be so bad if he did? Isn't that what you want—what you two are heading for?"

I swallowed a bite of ketchup-drenched sweet potato fry, beads of sweat forming on my forehead.

Maxie had a point. It wasn't as if I was too young. Twenty-eight was a perfectly reasonable age to get married. So why did I feel so anxious every time someone brought up the subject? The answer that immediately came caused a bit of phlegm to rise up in my throat.

"Yeah, maybe." I stared down at my plate, continuing to push the small cubes of tangy potatoes back and forth. "I just don't know if we're really right for each other, long term, Teddy and me." I looked up, my eyebrow cocked. "I told you about the disaster at The Hibiscus, right?"

Maxie nodded.

"Well, I just don't know if I'm up for an entire lifetime of that. And the whole time he just kept saying, 'Let's make the best of it, let's make the best of it.' Like, it was no big deal. Sometimes, I think he's just so…clueless."

Maxie took another slurp of her cocktail and leaned back in her chair, holding the drink beside her face. "Maybe there's nothing to worry about. Maybe he isn't going to propose. I mean, he's clearly in love with you and you *have* been dating for two years. But is there any other possibility as to why he planned this trip?"

I rolled my eyes and leaned my head toward Maxie. "There's no telling. I mean, last night he said he took me to The Hibiscus because it was the anniversary of the first time we had sex. Like I would remember that. He remembers everything."

Maxie snorted, almost spitting out the sip of drink she had just ingested. She was an artist, so she could afford to drink during the day. She painted stunning, oversized, vibrant pieces, but she had found fame doing what she called Found Object Art. She used things like hubcaps and half-used toothpaste tubes to create collage-style vignettes. They made a statement on the massive amount of trash Americans throw out each day while also being stunning. Her pieces had been shown throughout the country. She said alcohol only aided her process. Lucky bitch.

True to the artist cliche, Maxie didn't have a steady partner either. Instead, she kept several "lovers" on the line. This was an idea that intrigued me…but it just wasn't me. I had only had sex with one other guy before Teddy.

"That's…so Minnesota," Maxie said.

"Exactly."

"I don't mean that as an insult. It's earnest, cute."

"And, last night…it was almost sad. Like, we were seated next to the restroom and he had no power to change it. He even went to the hostess and asked her to move us, to no avail. I mean, is this as good as it's ever gonna get?"

Maxie used her sneaker to gently nudge my leg under the table.

"C'mon, what's wrong with you? Appreciate the poor guy. And, anyway, it's that underdog type that finds fame and fortune in the end. You just have to stick around long enough to find out. He *does* have his own kids' singing show on public television." She winked at me before bringing a forkful of salad to her mouth.

"Do you ever…" I paused, staring off in thought. "Well, no, not you—you're an artist with open relationships. But I—I sometimes feel a bit…"

"Spit it out."

"This isn't the way I imagined my life playing out. Teddy isn't the man I imagined for myself."

Maxie balanced her fork on the edge of her plate and cocked her head. "Okay. What did you imagine, exactly?"

I shrugged, my gaze sweeping the diamond-shaped blocks of sunlight shining through the lattice roof above us. "Plenty of people have found massive success at my age. I'm not even asking for that…"

"Is this about singing again, honey? I told you, you should do the open mic night at Cher Standley's. Give it a shot. Why not?"

My heart began pounding violently. "*No*. I can't even imagine that. I haven't sung in private in years, let alone in front of other people. You've never heard me sing, Teddy's hasn't either…and he's a singer himself."

Maxie dropped her eyes to her plate and took a slow inhale. Then she stretched out her arm and laid a well-moisturized hand over mine.

"Just try to appreciate the life you have. I know it sounds cliche, but…you don't know what you got until it's gone."

"No, you're right."

Theoretically, sure. But that didn't change the overwhelming annoyance I felt with Teddy and the rest of my life.

Maxie's phone began vibrating in her bag and she pulled it out.

"Ugh, sorry—I've got to go. I'm meeting with a potential supplier." She slid out from beneath the table, the loose skirt of her dress blowing in the wind. She walked over to my side and gave me a peck on the forehead. "Have fun this weekend." She wagged her finger at me. "You don't want to be eighty years old on your deathbed, regretting all the life you didn't appreciate."

I looked up at her, and we exchanged smiles. "I know you're right, bestie."

"Call me when you get back," she called over her shoulder.

I watched until she disappeared around the corner of the building.

A sinking feeling slowly began to creep over me. My lunches with Maxie were a breath of fresh air, an escape from the rest of my life. The problem was, they always came to an end.

I squeezed my eyes shut and massaged the area over my eyebrows with my index fingers, wondering how I was going to get through the rest of the day.

Chapter Three

Skye

"So how did you decide on this place?" I asked.

Teddy backed out of the driveway leading to his ranch-style house, our overnight bags crammed into the trunk. Despite my nerves, I was attempting to achieve what Maxie had urged me to do—to *live in the moment*—but so far I was finding that surprisingly difficult.

"It just seemed like what I was looking for," he said.

After my lunch with Maxie, I had returned to find the office in an even more frantic state. Francesca's mood had turned even more hateful.

"I hope you were out doing something to make Sissy's visit easier," she said after I took two steps in the door.

"No, I was…"

"She was running some errands for me," Dallas said.

It was almost irritating that a five-foot-eleven blonde former teen pop star was also nice. Still, I mouthed *thank you* as I hurried to my desk.

"I'm going to need you to stay out of the way," Francesca said.

I looked up, expecting her to be addressing all

three of us. Instead, she stared directly at me.

"Uh—oh-okay…"

I mostly succeeded in remaining invisible during Sissy's visit except for the one time the buxom singer and I crossed paths as I exited the bathroom. I had obediently kept my gaze down as Sissy's assistant had requested, except for one brief moment when I passed by her. I glanced up to find her sneering at me. It was a look that elicited shame. It made me feel even more like a peon than I already did—which was probably exactly what she intended.

Ever since that encounter, I had been ruminating over that look. How dare Sissy Stone sneer down her cosmetically-altered nose at me like I was a nobody—like I was someone who should kiss her toenail? We had both started out in the same place, on the same damn reality show. I mean, was she really that much better of a singer than me? Or had she just gotten lucky?

Teddy reached over and placed his hand over mine for a brief moment before returning it to the steering wheel. We were both pressed back against our seats as the car ascended a winding slope. I glanced through the glass at the softly rolling hills, accented with a few towering palm trees illuminated in the moonlight.

"You okay?" Teddy asked softly. "I feel like you're somewhere else."

I inhaled. "It was just a rough day at work. I'm fine."

"It seems like you're always somewhere else lately. Everything okay?"

"Yes, Teddy." My tone was unintentionally short.

A few minutes later, we pulled onto a secluded

drive bordered with thick, intertwining trees that formed a roof over us. A large wooden sign carved with the name "The Cypress Inn" sat at the road's edge.

As Teddy navigated down the tree-lined path, a multi-story Victorian building came into view. It featured several curved banisters, peaked rooftops accented with intricate tiled panels, and a dreamy second-story balcony. Meticulously maintained shrubbery bordered the large front porch and the leaves of a weeping birch tree hung around its front. It felt as if we were stepping back into the 1800s.

"How did you know about this place?" I leaned forward for a better view.

"I didn't." Teddy smiled over at me as he pulled into a parking spot. "I asked around. Caroline picked it out for us."

I flinched at the mention of his producer's name. *Blech.* I didn't want her to be any part of our romantic weekend…even if it was a weekend I had been dreading.

Teddy slid the key out of the ignition and turned to face me in the front seat. Beyond the Inn, a crisscross of white lights created a pseudo-roof over a sprawling terrace. It was bordered by towering, Alice in Wonderland style hedges.

"Wow, this place is beautiful," I said.

Teddy enveloped one of my hands between both of his. "I wanted to find somewhere we could be alone and just enjoy being together. An escape from all the craziness of L.A., without Francesca texting you or Caroline calling me…"

I smiled, my anxiety-ridden fears of an impending proposal momentarily overshadowed by my excitement to experience this beautiful retreat. Maybe a fun weekend was all this would be…maybe I was worrying over nothing.

After we had checked in with the friendly front desk clerk, a charming bellhop in a square hat delivered our suitcases to the suite. As Teddy tipped him, I examined the space.

A large four-poster bed was flanked with ivory draperies, an embroidered comforter, and a wooden headboard carved with diamond shapes. An upholstered fainting chair sat next to a glass table, which held a bottle of champagne and two glasses. I swallowed, the hairs on the back of my neck standing up as I considered the implications of that champagne.

Beyond the enormous four-poster bed, two French doors led to a balcony. They were accented with matching ornate wooden trim and carved glass. A large statue depicting the Buddha in a meditative pose sat just inside on a small table.

After the bellhop left, Teddy strode across the room, opened the balcony doors, and held out his hand.

"Care to join me?"

I crossed the distance between us and stepped outside. A balmy breeze danced across our faces as I took in the stunning patio below, obscured by the intersecting white lights above it. Teddy grasped my hip and pressed his mouth into my hair.

"I'm taking you out tonight, Peters."

I sniffed, keeping my eyes on a group of cypress trees in the distance stretching their limbs toward the darkening sky.

"Oh, yeah? Where to?"

"Right here. They have a world-class restaurant

downstairs. That was part of the appeal of this place."

I turned to look at him, our faces inches apart. "You're a big spender lately. That's not like you." I tilted my head.

Teddy squeezed my hip as he gazed into my eyes. "You just bring it out in me." He winked. "Our reservations are in half an hour, actually. Want to get dressed? You can have the bathroom. I know how you like your privacy."

"Okay, sure."

I swept back into the room, scooped up my printed overnight bag, and shut the bathroom door behind me. Blessed privacy, indeed. I was happy to be alone for at least a moment. I exhaled a breath I didn't know I had been holding, dropped my bag onto the white tiled floor, and glanced around.

The space was roomy, with a jacuzzi tub enveloped in the same carved wood panels as the bed. There was a separate shower, double sinks, and a water closet. I stuck my head inside a door beside the water closet and found an actual closet. It was equipped with a long metal bar holding a few bare hangers.

I spun around, pressed my palms against the cool granite counter, and stared into the mirror. "You can do this."

I hastily undressed, rinsed off in a five-minute shower, updated my lipstick to a deep matte red, and added liquid liner to my already mascara-ed eyes. I stepped into a red dress with a swooping back and wrapped a shawl around my shoulders. Finally, I inhaled deeply through my nose and stepped out of the bathroom, expecting to find Teddy. But the room was empty.

"I'm out here," a disjointed voice called.

Dropping my shawl on the chair, I walked over to the opened French doors. Teddy was leaning against the balcony railing. He was more dressed up than usual, which made me deeply wary. His slightly shiny button-down shirt was tucked into sleek gray slacks. He scanned my body before meeting my eyes.

"Wow," he breathed. "I like this bold color choice. You look incredible." He leaned forward and pressed his lips against mine.

"So do you," I said once he pulled away.

"See? No khakis." He wrapped an arm around my bare ones and pulled me close.

"Very nice…I see you're wearing one of the pairs I picked out for you. Finally."

The suddenly cooler air chilled my bare skin, making me yearn for the shawl I'd left inside. I let my weight fall against Teddy and gazed at a couple strolling slowly hand-in-hand across the manicured lawn.

I was drifting into a slightly calmer state when Teddy pulled away. I wobbled for a moment, catching my balance. The energy between us seemed to change abruptly into something heavier.

No. Please, God, no.

He turned to face me and positioned my body so it mirrored his own. I swallowed the lump in my throat. My heart beat so violently it shook my frame.

I was twenty-eight. Teddy was thirty…it made sense he would want more. That he would want a family. That I should.

"Do you remember the first night we met, Peters?" he asked.

I pictured the dark dance club, the cool air on my sweaty skin, the pulsating beat of a song being played too loud in a good way.

"I was thinking about that," he said. "The first night I saw you. You were—are—incredible. Honestly, waiting this long has been hard. I wanted to do it a few months after I met you. Aiden is the one who encouraged me to slow down. So I did. But waiting this long to ask you has been one of the hardest things I've ever had to do."

Teddy's hand moved to the pocket of his slacks. I suddenly noticed the outline of a small, square object. His fingers gripped the item and, as he started to pull it out, I saw the edge of a blue velvet box.

Perspiration beaded on my brow. I had the sense that something was tightening around my neck, squeezing my throat. My face tingled as air seemed to fill my head. I struggled to swallow. My inhales became shallower and shallower until I was practically hyperventilating.

Teddy's knee began to bend.

"I don't feel so good." I grasped the metal railing for support.

Teddy's knee straightened as he placed his hand on my arm. "What's wrong?"

"I just—I need some air." I gestured at my throat and waved my hand frantically.

"Okay. But…we're outside."

"Then…I need *less* air." I turned and ran into the room, looking back once I crossed the threshold. "I'm fine. I just need to be alone for a minute."

A shadow fell over Teddy's face and the corners of his mouth drooped. He gave a small nod. My heart ached for him, but I couldn't make it better. I couldn't stop the way I felt.

"Thanks," I called, racing towards the bathroom. I slammed the door shut behind me.

I paced back and forth on the tile floor, glancing at myself in the mirror. A small woman in a bright red dress, hunched forward and frantic with distress. I flinched, looking away.

My sense of breathlessness wasn't improving. I fought the urge to burst through the door and out into the night, purely due to some sense of vanity. I didn't want to make a total fool of myself. So I wandered to the closet, instinctively feeling as if being cocooned inside of a small space would provide a sense of relief. A womb-like comfort.

Then there was a knock on the bathroom door.

"Are you okay in there?"

I waved my hand as if Teddy could see me. "I'm fine."

I dove into the closet and shut the door behind me. I pulled my legs tight to my chest and wrapped my arms around them. The fetal position. I sensed a tickle behind my eyes, and wet, soggy tears soon began cutting lines through my makeup.

The idea of getting engaged to Teddy—it absolutely terrified me. Why couldn't I just be happy about it? Why couldn't I just be like every other woman seemed to be? The idea of marriage made me feel as if I were inside of a vise grip, the walls closing in around me. I desperately wanted to get out, to get away. I simply couldn't stomach the thought of a life of mediocrity. And isn't that what I would be settling for?

Lacking the energy to crawl out of the closet to the

toilet paper roll, I grabbed the hem of my crimson dress and rubbed it beneath each eye.

"Skye? Will you let me in, please?"

"Stop talking," I hissed under my breath.

Though my plea was likely too quiet for Teddy to hear, a prolonged silence followed. I cocked my ear toward the door, waiting. Was he angry? Distraught?

Finally, I heard Teddy speaking, but it was from somewhere deep within the room. It sounded as if he was talking to someone else. But to whom? Had the bellhop returned?

As I listened, unable to make out his exact words, Teddy's tone turned from calm to angry. At first, I thought he was talking to himself. But then I heard a scuffle, as if two or more people were fighting. Something was knocked over, then it sounded as if someone was shoved hard against the wall.

My body tensed. "Teddy?" I called.

As I got to my feet and reached for the doorknob, I heard it: the sound of a gunshot. I couldn't be sure, as I'd heard the sound in person so rarely. But the sickening firecracker pop was identical to what I'd heard in movies and on television.

The bathroom door creaked ominously open. I froze in place.

The heavy groan of footsteps that weren't Teddy's moved closer before I heard the water closet door beside me creak open. I pressed myself against the wall.

Everything was silent for a moment. Then the closet door burst open, revealing a terrifying sight. An imposing figure in a knit face mask. He was wearing black gloves and pointing an awful silver gun in my direction.

I dove toward the other side of the closet. The intruder roughly yanked me up, shoved me hard against the closet wall, and aimed the gun at me again. Another awful pop of gunfire, then piercing pain permeated my left arm. I screamed, my voice sounding like a wounded animal to my own ears.

As I dropped to the ground grasping my arm, a shadow caused me to look up. Teddy emerged from behind the man, holding the heavy Buddha statue over his head. Baring his teeth, Teddy dropped the piece hard on the masked man's skull. The intruder dropped to the floor with a loud thud.

As Teddy moved toward me, the piercing pain seemed to ease. Then everything went black.

Chapter Four

Caroline - Two weeks earlier

I sat at my desk in the dim, cool darkness of the *Tunes by Teddy* studio, drenched in the blue light of my computer screen. It was eight-fifteen on a Friday morning and, as we filmed on Thursdays, the calmest day of the week. It was the day when the satisfaction of accomplishing another show was at its highest and the frenzied chaos that built before it was sublimely low.

The cavernous studio around me was mostly empty. The little red lights on the blocky cameras were black and the only people I spotted were two production assistants conversing quietly in a corner.

I brought half of a cream-cheese-smeared bagel to my lips and used my index finger to scroll down on the mouse. I paused my scrolling at a headline that caught my attention and pressed play. I took a slow slip of my whipped-cream-topped mocha latte and watched.

The video showed the vain, vapid pop star Sissy Stone posing on a red carpet in a sparkly mini-dress. I scoffed, rolling my eyes.

What a perfect example of an ignorant little twit. Los Angeles was filled with them: identical blonde morons foaming at the mouth to become known, no matter what they had to do to achieve it. Fame and fortune over self-respect and service.

It was pathetic.

I would never have moved to Burbank if it hadn't been for Ted. It didn't matter that I hadn't actually met him yet when I made the decision to relocate from New York. I knew, *just knew,* after I saw him that first time on television: we were meant to be together.

"Hey, Caroline. Do you have a minute?"

The heady, intoxicating timbre of Ted's voice wafted toward me. He wasn't usually in this early on Fridays. My body lifted from the rolling chair like the nose of a dog catching the scent of red meat.

I glanced over to find him smiling a lopsided grin as he gestured toward his office. It was during loaded moments like this I felt certain he knew it too. There was something between us. Something big. Something monumental.

"Sure, of course, yes. Be right there."

I watched as he walked away. Then I hastily dotted the corners of my mouth and yanked open the top drawer of my desk. I pulled out a small mirror and examined my teeth. I raked a hand through my dirty blonde pixie cut until I was satisfied, then swiped peachy gloss across my lips. That would have to do. Our bond was light years beyond the physical, anyway.

"Shut the door, please," Ted said from behind his desk as I entered. I did as he said and went to perch in one of the two chairs situated opposite him. "I need your advice."

Ted looked handsome of course. His cheerful face was slightly tanner than normal, and his lively brown eyes were even livelier. My cheeks ached, I was beaming so widely.

I crossed my legs, leaned my elbow on the edge of

his desk, and cocked my head. I gave him my most concerned expression. *Tell me, Ted. Tell me everything.*

"I'm going to ask her." Ted's voice was low and serious. "I'm going to ask Skye to marry me."

His perfect mouth burst into a smile as my breakfast threatened to come up. I watched in horror as he slid a tiny blue ring box from his pocket and flipped it open. A brilliant oval diamond surrounded by smaller diamonds sat perched on a pale blue velvet cushion.

"What do you think?"

Skye Peters was not supposed to get that ring. I was. The ring in that little blue box was supposed to be mine. I imagined swiping the awful thing from Ted's palm, bursting out of the door, and chucking it into a passing garbage truck. That was where it truly belonged. I wanted that atrocity out of my sight as quickly as possible.

I stood with as much class as I could muster and turned on my heel.

"Where are you going?"

"Bad bagel or something," I called once I was safely outside the office door. "I think I'm going to be sick."

I ran-walked through the darkened studio and slammed open the swinging women's restroom door. Luckily, the rest of the bathroom was silent. I kicked open one of the hideous electric blue stall doors and locked it shut behind me. Then I ripped out a handful of the scratchy industrial toilet paper and dotted the tears moistening my cheeks. I had to gain control of my racing thoughts. I had to figure this out.

This wasn't supposed to happen. How could Ted be so…so—no, I wouldn't blame him. It wasn't his fault. It was all due to that blonde zombie, a woman identical to so many others in this God-forsaken city. She had brainwashed him, pure and simple. Bamboozled him. I wouldn't let this happen. I wouldn't let her become Mrs. Sorens.

As the awful phrase ripped through my body—Mrs. Skye Sorens—I sat down on the toilet seat and dropped my head between my knees. Ted was supposed to be my saving grace, my brighter future. If he wasn't part of my tomorrow, where did that leave me?

I tossed the damp toilet paper in the trash, wiped my still-wet cheeks with the back of my hand, and took a slow, deep inhale.

No. I would not take this lying down. I would not play nice. I would do everything in my power to stop Ted from marrying Skye.

Straightening my hunched spine and pushing back my aching shoulders, I strode back to Ted's office. He was standing behind his desk, his dark eyes filled with concern.

"Can I come in?" I asked.

"Of course."

Ted walked around the desk toward me and sat in the adjacent chair. As he leaned forward and rested his arm behind me, I caught the scent of his Armani cologne and pine-scented soap. There was a faint layer of stubble on his cheeks. Being so close made me feel as if someone had flipped the "on" switch in my body. I was suddenly alive.

God, I wanted to jump his bones right there.

"What's going on, Caroline?" His voice was low and soft.

I swallowed, chewing on my bottom lip.

This was my chance. I had to go for it. I had to put it all on the line. It might be the only way to make our destiny unfold as it was meant to.

I placed a hand lightly on Ted's knee. He glanced down and adjusted in his seat, his body stiffening.

"What's going on is that I love you. Can you not see that?"

Ted's mouth fell open, but no words came out.

"I love you," I repeated.

Then I did it. I leaned forward and pressed my lips hard against his. I felt his stubble against my skin, a pleasurable kind of pain, and tasted the incredible flavor of him. Though he didn't kiss me back, he didn't immediately pull away either. That was something. That was progress.

"Did you not feel that?" I sat back and squeezed Ted's knee. "Tell me you did."

An abrupt knock at the door interrupted us. We both turned to see a production assistant poke his head inside. The man's face went slack when he saw us so close together. A feeling of satisfaction seeped through me.

"Excuse me," the PA said, backing away.

Ted sprang up, waving his hands in the air. "No, no, come in. Please."

As the man entered, Ted looked down at me. "Can you give us a minute?"

Hesitantly, I stood and ambled toward the door. The assistant stepped aside to let me pass. I sensed the eyes of Ted and the man drilling into the back of my head as I moved in the direction of my desk.

Sitting down, the image of Skye immediately bludgeoned me. Her glossy blonde hair. Her clueless blue eyes. The thought of her and Ted spending an eternity together. It made me sick.

I was proud of myself. I had done what needed to be done. If Ted still made a bad decision—the worst decision he could possibly make—and married that cardboard cut-out of a woman, at least I would have tried.

And yet. Trying wasn't enough. I stared at my computer screen, unseeing, and made a decision. I wouldn't let her win. I would stop at nothing to prevent this disaster from occurring.

I would make her pay for what she had done.

Chapter Five

Skye

I was falling. I plummeted through the air for several seconds, landing with a *thud* on a thickly piled, cream-colored rug.

I looked around, head spinning. I immediately spotted something red on the ground next to me and grabbed it. It was the dress I had just been wearing. What the hell?

I glanced down at myself, expecting to see my naked body—and blood. Lots of blood. Instead, I saw I was wearing an off-the-shoulder sweatshirt and expensive-looking gray sweatpants. The skin I could see was clean and dry, free from any blood at all.

I expanded my line of vision, taking in my surroundings. I seemed to have fallen into the middle of a stunning, sun-filled living room. In front of me was a large living area with a white sectional, an art deco glass end table, and a massive wall-mounted television. To my left was a wall of windows revealing a patio beyond. I squinted: was that…the Hollywood hills?

Oh my God. Was this it? Had I been murdered? Was one of Jesus's angelic assistants going to walk out to greet me next?

I glanced upwards, expecting to see the closet from which I had just plummeted…but I didn't. Instead, there were hundred-foot ceilings and double-paned skylights above a sprawling staircase. What was happening to me?

I scanned the floor around me, searching for debris from the closet, from the gunshot. There was nothing but spotless floors.

"Teddy?" I squeaked. "Are you here?"

I shakily stood up, aware of a growing sense of unease. Nothing I saw made any sense. Yet, I was conscious—wasn't I? Is this what it felt like to be dead? Shouldn't I have a sense of calm or something? My heart began to pound erratically.

I was afraid to walk forward or backward—to take a step in any direction. So I sat back down, curled up into the fetal position, and squeezed my eyes shut.

"None of this is real, I'm back in the closet, I just invented this as an escape from my reality..."

I opened one eye to look around. Still in the sun-filled living room. *Oh, God.* I closed my eyes again and slowly inhaled and exhaled, rocking back and forth.

"Skye? Are you okay? What the hell are you doin'?"

A man's gravelly voice—vaguely familiar, but definitely not Teddy's—was suddenly speaking to me. I unclenched and lifted my head up, searching. The man stood beside the staircase in a large tiled foyer leading to two oversized glass-paned front doors. He gazed at me with something resembling amusement, one eyebrow cocked slightly.

It took a moment, but I recognized him: it was the man from the photos with Sissy Stone. What was his name?

"Mark Campbell," I said aloud.

His eyebrow dropped back into place as his mouth formed a wide, closed-lipped smile.

"That's me." His thick Scottish accent made the "me" sound more like "may."

"You're not real."

Mark's smile vanished as he came to crouch beside me. He put his fingers lightly on my shoulder.

"Is this about the blog article yesterday? I told you, any press is good press. And they're just looking for something to fill up their content. It's nothing for you to get upset over. And not a bit of truth to it." He put a hand under my armpit, which caused me to jump, and began pulling me up. "Come on. Up we go."

I shoved him away, sliding back on the floor. "Who are you? What is going on here?"

Mark, or at least the man who looked like Mark, lifted his eyebrow again, pushed out his lips, and turned the corners of his mouth downward. "Skye, c'mon. Get it together. Should I get you one of your happy pills?"

I was unsure if I had ever taken one of these so-called happy pills before—maybe after a dental surgery a few years back. Still, I instinctively answered in the affirmative.

"Yes. Please."

Mark stood and peered down, squinting at me. "Can you at least go and lie on the couch?"

I considered this for a moment before pushing myself to my feet. Whatever would make the man leave and go get me the happy pills, I would do.

I sunk into the sofa in the living room, its cushions feeling like clouds themselves—oh, shit, maybe this *was* heaven. The man calling himself Mark brought me a pretty little pill and a glass of water.

"Can I get a glass of wine too? Preferably a Cab?" I asked.

I wanted anything to numb these waves of anxiety. And, if I was a goner anyway, why hold back?

Mark's face morphed into amusement again. He stared at me with a knowing sparkle in his eyes. "How 'bout we just stick with the pills for now? Huh, Freckles?"

At the sound of his apparent nickname for me, my heart flip-flopped. I absentmindedly brought my fingers to the dusting of freckles at my nose. The name sounded so intimate. I popped the pill into my mouth and downed the glass of water.

I must have dozed off shortly after that. I was vaguely aware of Mark disappearing and appearing beside me again. When the sun was gone and the windows were dark, Mark slid his strong arms beneath me and hoisted me off the couch. I struggled weakly, but, feeling exhausted, swiftly gave up.

"Let's get you to bed," he said, his face close to mine.

"Put me down. I was fine where I was…"

Mark bypassed the staircase and instead carried me inside a waiting elevator, then out into a massive master suite. He laid me on top of a bed even softer than the couch, pulling a silky comforter over me.

"Try to get some sleep." His voice was low and husky.

"I don't know what's going on here." I struggled to sit up. "But I'm not okay with it. I don't belong here. I need to get back—to my boyfriend. He's going to be wondering where I am. And he might be in trouble."

Mark paused, clenching his jaw and furrowing his

brow. "Your *boyfriend*?"

"Yes…"

I looked across the bed and noticed flickering flames in a fireplace. Okay, so if this guy *was* holding me hostage, it could have been worse. Still, I had to get the hell out of there.

"Huh."

Mark considered my statement for a moment, then sat on the edge of the bed.

"What's going on here, Skye? Are you trying to tell me something?"

I let out an impatient sigh. "Yes. I have no idea where I am, and my boyfriend, Ted Sorens, is going to be wondering where I am. Can I please borrow a phone?" I glanced around me on the bed. "I have no idea where mine is."

"Can I have *your boyfriend's* number? I'll give him a call."

"Yes." I recited Teddy's number.

Mark slid a large phone from his trouser pocket and tapped into the glass screen with his thumb. "And what should I tell him?" Mark brought the phone to his ear. "That you're with your husband? Will that ease his mind?"

At the word "husband," I dropped my gaze to examine my hands. The largest diamond I had ever seen glittered on my left ring finger. It was square-shaped and massive, sparkling magnificently in the firelight. I twisted my neck to examine the bedside table. There was a photo of Mark and me on what appeared to be our wedding day. I wore a gorgeous white strapless gown, and Mark was debonair in a tux. It all looked so real.

"This is Mark Campbell. Is this Ted…Sorens?…Great." Mark's tone was sarcastic. He handed me the phone, narrowing his eyes. "I'll let you talk to him."

I struggled to catch my breath. "Teddy? Is that you? Thank God…"

I listened for Teddy's familiar voice. "Yes? Who am I speaking to?"

"Teddy. It's me. It's Skye."

Another confused pause. "Skye?"

"Skye *Peters?*"

Confused silence.

Finally Teddy spoke. "The pop star? Oh, wow, my niece loves you…did I win something or…?"

"Pop star? What? Teddy, I need your help."

"Wait, there's no way this is really Skye Peters. Nice try." *Click.*

I dropped the phone on the bed and checked the number to confirm Mark had truly called Teddy. He had.

Something cold began to trickle through my veins, beginning at the roots of my hair and flowing into my toenails.

"Satisfied?" Mark scooped up the phone. "Do I need to call Dr. Jones? I really don't want her visit getting leaked to the press—again."

"No, don't call anybody." The last thing I needed was to be drugged by some psychiatrist to the stars.

"Listen." Mark stood. "I didn't want to leave you today—but I really need to get some work done. Are you going to be okay on your own for a little while?"

I glanced at the clock on the bedside table. 10:31 p.m. Odd time for the office.

"Yes. I'll be fine. Go."

Mark stared at me for a moment, as if he was deciding whether to believe me or not. Then he started toward the door, turning back once before vanishing from the room.

I had the urge to curl up into the fetal position again and squeeze my eyes shut until things started to make sense. Had I been shot through the heart? Was this purgatory? Or—heaven? Either way, I wasn't ready to die. And I needed answers.

Before I could ponder my fate much longer, I must have passed out again because I didn't awaken until something bright was shining in my eyes.

****

I was in the middle of a vivid dream. My grandmother, Sharon, who died three years earlier, was holding something out to me. It was odd-shaped and unrecognizable. Still, I knew instinctively—it was a gift. Just before I opened my eyes, her sweet, familiar voice echoed in my ears.

"Don't look a gift horse in the mouth," she said. "Just *accept it. Accept it. Accept it.*"

My eyes surged open onto the same luxurious master suite, now as sun-filled as the living room had been the day before.

"Is she dead?"

I twisted my neck. A small boy of about eight was standing next to the bed. He had dark hair and eyes. A girl of about twelve appeared beside him.

"No," she said. "Unfortunately not."

Another voice caused me to abruptly sit up.

"Kids. Get out!"

A blonde woman appeared behind them in the

doorway. I glanced at her—then looked again. Was it—*no way.*

"Dallas?"

"Yes, hey. *Sorry.* Shoo-shoo." She waved her hands behind the children, herding them toward the door. The boy left without issue, but the girl paused and shot me a withering look before vanishing. "*She's here*," Dallas hissed.

I wasn't sure who "she" was, but I had more pressing issues to discuss with my coworker.

"Dallas, I'm so happy to see you. You have no idea how worried I've been."

Dallas grabbed a chair from behind an ornate, light pink vanity and dragged it across the floor until it was beside the bed.

"Yes, so sorry I'm late."

She crossed her legs, opened up a notebook, and held a pen above it, waiting.

I expected her to say more, but she was silent. "Do you have any idea what's going on here?" I widened my eyes at her for added impact.

Dallas looked one way, then the other. "What do you mean?"

I relaxed, eliciting a snort of laughter. "I was starting to freak out. So thank God you're here."

Dallas furrowed her brow and cocked her head. A look of understanding spread over her features.

"Oh." She elongated the word as if she suddenly understood. "Is this about the Sonny Music Awards?"

"What? What about the Sonny Awards?"

A line appeared between Dallas' eyebrows. She laid a hand on my arm. "You're up for three awards…remember?"

My body went cold.

"Dallas, we're coworkers. We work at Pepperlake PR together. Francesca Shaw is our boss."

Dallas scoffed. "Our boss? Francesca Shaw? Your PR person? Why would she ever be considered *our boss*? She works for you."

I squeezed my eyes shut and saw my grandmother's image holding out the odd-shaped object. Maybe this *was* some sort of gift from God. Maybe the only way around it was through it. Sure, whatever. I would play along for now.

"Look around." Dallas smiled. "You're a world-famous, Sonny-winning musician, married to a wonderfully talented music producer." She paused, her shockingly white teeth on display as she beamed at me. "There's no need to pretend to be anyone else, period. *Now.* Let's get going."

Dallas stared down at the notebook in her lap.

"Yes, of course," I said. "I'm just…*p-p-processing* some things. So, how did we meet again?"

"Oh." Dallas tilted her head, glanced to the left, and brought the pen she was holding to her lips. "It must have been…at the MTV Music Awards. I was on my way down in the industry, and it was your first time at the show. You completely owned the night—it was your knockout performance in the black lace teddy, right?"

"Yes…that sounds like me."

"Is she still in bed? *Gah.*"

A nasally female voice caused us both to look toward the door. A tiny brunette woman stood with her arms crossed over her chest. Her shiny hair was pulled up into a tight ponytail and she wore oversized sunglasses. Her curves were on full display in athletic wear. It took me a minute, but I quickly realized why she seemed so familiar. It was the woman I'd seen on the video with Mark, pivoting in a red evening gown. His estranged wife.

"Excuse me, JoJo." Dallas hurried to the door. "I'm going to have to request privacy for Skye."

"Ha!" JoJo scoffed. "Like we haven't all seen it before. Look, missy. I'm dropping my children off and their father is nowhere to be found—big surprise. So I'm going to need a responsible adult to take charge if I am to, in good conscience, leave them here. Would your client care to get out of bed and get dressed? My children will be needing lunch soon."

She spoke to Dallas as if she were speaking to a three-year-old. Dallas glanced back at me, her eyebrows lifted expectantly.

"Oh, yes." I struggled to get out from beneath the covers. "I'll just, um, be down in a few seconds."

JoJo glared pointedly over her sunglasses. Then she spun on her heel and disappeared. Dallas shut the door.

"So sorry about that," she said. "I had no idea they were coming today. It wasn't on the schedule. Did Mark say—"

"No." My blood pressure was rising. "Whose kids are those? And what am I supposed to do with them?"

Dallas took a breath. "Oh, okay, we're still doing this. Those kids are your stepchildren, Lucienne and Comet, from your marriage to Mark."

I glanced again at the wedding photo I'd spotted last night. My face glowed in the image as I held the hand of Mark, my apparent husband. Mark's shockingly handsome face was alight with love. He *was* sexy…

"Was it an…acrimonious split between them?" I asked.

"Ummmm." Dallas bit her lip.

"That's okay. I'll just Wikipedia it."

I was proud of myself, taking this completely bizarre situation into my own hands, even just a bit. "By the way, where is my phone?"

"I'll track that down for you. In the meantime, let's get you dressed so we can get Mr. Campbell's ex-wife *out of here.*"

I followed Dallas around the corner of the bedroom into a cavernous closet. It displayed floor-to-ceiling clothes on every side, with an entire wall of shoes illuminated with individual lights (did I really wear heels that high?) and another wall stocked with handbags. I stepped closer to examine one that caught my eye. Holy shit…it was a Birkin. A fifty-thousand-dollar handbag.

"Let's see, we still need to get some shots in that new designer look. Why don't you wear this today?"

Dallas reached to a top rack holding a variety of clothing in pastel hues and pulled down a flowy jumpsuit. "Comfortable and still chic. You can wear it with the new wedge sandals Dior sent you."

After I was dressed in the green jumpsuit and sandals, Dallas spoke again.

"I gave Brenda the morning off. I figure we can do a fresh-faced look for today. I can do it for you, if you want."

I paused in front of a gilded mirror mounted over one of the bathroom sinks, confused. "Do what?"

"Your makeup, silly."

"Oh…right. Um, let's do that later…after we feed the kids." It felt so weird saying it. I had *kids?*

"You're right. We do need to get *her* out of here."

I trailed Dallas down the spiral staircase, past the foyer, and into the gleaming kitchen. I hadn't seen the space the previous night. Now I could see it was just as impressive as the rest of the house. There was an eight-burner gas stove with a glistening steel hood, an impossibly large granite-topped island, and a wall of windows surrounding a breakfast nook.

"Well, well. So nice of you to join us." JoJo stood in a corner, one leg cocked to the side. She briefly lifted her eyes from her phone, then dropped them back again. Her dark sunglasses had been shoved to the top of her head and she held a large handbag that seemed even larger in comparison to her tiny frame. Lucienne and Comet sat at a table in the breakfast nook.

"Yes, sorry, we're—" Dallas started.

"Can *she* speak?" JoJo spat.

They both waited.

"So sorry to keep you waiting," I said. "Please feel free to go. I'll make sure the kids get a nutritious meal."

Lucienne snorted derisively as JoJo let out an exhausted sigh.

"Just tell Mark to be here when I pick the kids up tomorrow. I need to discuss their school schedules with him."

"Okay, sure. Of course."

Using her index finger, JoJo tipped the sunglasses back onto her nose and peered at me over them. Never taking her eyes off of me, she kissed each of her kids on the head, then swept dramatically out of the room.

"So," I said, after the front door clicked shut. "What would you kids like to eat?"

"Not hungry," Lucienne said. At the same time, Comet replied, "Fries!"

"Okay." I turned, expecting to see a fridge, but there was not one to be found. I searched up and down the wall of custom-made cabinets, peered around the corner into the small bedroom-sized pantry, and did a spin around the kitchen. "Um…."

"What is wrong with her?" Lucienne stuck out her bottom lip.

"No, nothing," I sung out.

I turned my back to the kids and leaned toward Dallas conspiratorially. "Where is the fridge?"

Dallas's eyes widened. If she hadn't been worried about me before, it seemed she was changing her mind.

"Right here." She stepped forward and pulled open one of the cabinets, revealing a clean, spectacularly organized freezer—presumably, the refrigerator side was on the right.

"Oh, they're *built-in.*" I glanced discreetly at Lucienne, who was glaring at me. "Well, I don't see any fries, Comet. But there are some tater tots."

"Blech," Comet said. "Can't Raphael make something?"

I glanced at Dallas, questioningly.

"Your personal chef," she whispered in reply. Then to Comet, "No, he's off on the weekends. Remember?"

Before I could flail around any longer, Dallas whipped out her phone and placed an order at a local brunch place. The food was delivered within fifteen minutes. Soon after, Lucienne and Comet were finished eating and licking their greasy fingers.

Insisting I stay seated, Dallas cleared the table. She gathered the trash in her arms, carried everything to the waste bin, and came to stand beside me.

"I think I'll take the kids for frozen yogurt," she said. "That'll give you a little time to yourself and—it seems like you could use it."

"When is Dad going to be home?" Lucienne asked, a whine in her voice.

Dallas glanced discreetly at me, waiting for my reply. When she saw I had no earthly idea, she spoke. "Soon, I'm sure. I think he was meeting with a client."

Once the kids had been successfully herded out the door, I made a beeline to the Mac desktop I had spotted in an adjacent office earlier.

I had only one goal: to figure out who the hell I was in this strange new world.

Chapter Six

Skye

Luckily, the password I needed to access the computer was scribbled out on a pink sticky note next to the keyboard. "SkyeLUVSMark467."

I navigated to Google and typed my name in the search box. I expected to see the usual semi-flattering profile photo of myself from Twitter and Instagram. But something miraculous happened. Just like everything else in this insane new world, the results surprised me.

The first was from a popular celebrity gossip magazine. It was a story featuring highly stylized photos of Mark and me posing around our house. *This* house. It was a full-on celebrity home tour. In the first shot, my bare legs were on display as I perched coquettishly on the arm of the sofa, a hand on Mark's shoulder. The second shot showed me at a bar, holding up a flute to the camera as I tilted to the side playfully.

I clicked out and scanned to the second search result. It was for my Wikipedia page. *Jackpot*. I began scanning the sections. Early Life, Career, Achievements…

As I perused the career section, my heart dropped into my stomach. I fell back in my chair. It said I had won *Countdown to Famous*. Sissy had come in third. I didn't even recognize the name of the person in second place. It also said I had been Louie Topherson's darling—that he'd gone to bat for me against the other judges.

Louie Topherson? The same man who had battered my will to sing beyond recognition? How was this possible?

Another section reported that I'd made three albums and my eagerly anticipated fourth, "The Juice of a Thousand Melons," was soon to be released.

If this was what going crazy—or being dead—felt like, maybe it wasn't so bad.

Before I could peruse any further, a sharp beep pulled my attention to the corner of the room. I suddenly noticed a smartphone resting in a charging station. Mine? I ran to it and swiped it up. After several tries, I correctly guessed the password: "Mark." The alternate me seemed to be quite taken with this man.

The newly unlocked phone elicited a series of dings and pings as the screen filled up with notification after notification. I was alerted to an endless barrage of text messages and missed calls. I spotted the Instagram app and opened it.

My breath caught in my throat as I clutched the phone. Was it even possible to have so much activity? A string of alerts told me someone had liked my latest post, or the post before that. The alerts never stopped. I finally ceased scrolling and clicked onto my account. The last photo was of Mark and me. It appeared we were dining at an outdoor patio, goofy grins on our faces. My head rested on his shoulder. We looked very much in love.

"Can't get enough of these tacos," the caption read,

followed by a series of heart-eye, taco, and drooling emojis.

I scanned the number beneath the photo. It had to be an error. I squeezed my eyes shut, letting the numbers go blurry before coming back into focus. No, there was no mistaking: the number was 983,456—just short of a million likes. Holy moly.

I decided to try an experiment. Looking down at my gorgeously painted coral toenails, I knew what my focus would be. I held one leg out in front of me, hovering above the floor. The bright wall of windows was evident beyond. *Click.* I didn't even take the time to edit it. I simply uploaded the pedicure pic, added a caption ("Love my latest color"), and posted it to Instagram. It wasn't two seconds before the first like came in, followed by a "They're gorgeous" comment. Then a barrage of more likes, ticking up my count to 300 in the first five minutes. I didn't recognize anyone's usernames.

This was highly addictive. I scanned the room for more ideas to shoot. Suddenly, a low baritone caused a chill down my spine.

"What are you doing in here, Freckles? I hardly ever see you in this part of the house."

I spun in the chair. Mark leaned against the doorway, a leg propped out to the side and a hand in his pocket. He wore a tight black henley and expensive-looking jeans. I had to admit, his Scottish accent was damn distracting.

"I hope you're feeling better today?" he said.

"Yes, um…better."

Mark strode confidently across the office in my direction, his intoxicating scent—something like freshly washed skin and earthy soap—enveloping my senses. He placed a hand firmly on the edge of the desk and leaned in. My body tensed at his closeness. He truly was a beautiful man. Six-foot-three-ish, with wide shoulders, thick brown hair, and curious eyes that seemed to drink you in. And evidently he was mine. He wanted *me*.

"I'm taking you out to The Hibiscus tonight after you're done. I want you all to myself." He winked, placing his imposing hands on my shoulders and gazing into my eyes. "I know I've been neglecting you lately. Maybe that's what last night was all about. Either way, I'm whisking you away."

His breath in my face was sweet as he let one hand skim my arm, his fingertips trailing against my uncovered skin. He leaned closer. I could see the variations of brown in his eyes. Before I could react, he pressed his mouth against mine, his lips slightly parted. I somehow managed not to leap out of my chair. Still, it felt like cheating on Teddy—even if Teddy apparently had no idea who I was in this alternate world.

The thought of my boyfriend caused an ache in my chest. I had hurt him, broken his heart maybe. The last time I had seen him he was attempting to rescue me from an intruder. *Dear God, please let Teddy be safe.* Was he okay? Alive? Was I? I had been shot. I'd heard the gunfire, felt the sharp, piercing pain of the bullet penetrating my flesh.

Maybe that explained all of this. Maybe I was lying unconscious in a hospital room right now.

Mark pulled away.

"Got to go, Love. More of that later." He smiled suggestively, then turned and strode back out of the door.

I exhaled. Mark's presence was overwhelming. As I was taking several shaky inhales, the voices of Dallas, Lucienne, and Comet wafted into the room. I stood and wandered toward the foyer. The kids were already halfway up the stairs.

"Hi, guys," I called.

Neither of them responded so I went into the kitchen. Dallas was placing her pillbox purse onto the table in the breakfast nook.

"Mark left?" Dallas asked.

"Yes. He, uh, he's taking me to dinner tonight."

Dallas nodded briskly. "So you'll head straight to dinner after the concert venue?"

"We're going to a concert too? He didn't mention anything about that."

Dallas smiled as if she thought I was telling a joke. "Right…no, *your* concert."

I became aware of a hollowed-out feeling in my stomach. My heart instantly started pounding so hard I feared it might beat right out of my chest. "What? *No*."

Dallas looked up at me from her phone, a line between her brows. "You forgot?" she asked gently.

I clutched the edge of the cold countertop with both hands. My knuckles turned white. "I can't sing in front of people…how many people?"

Dallas walked over to me and laid her hand gently on my arm. "Are you feeling panicky again? I really do think we should call Dr. Jones. There's nothing wrong with taking medication when it's warranted. I understand Mark's worry, but—"

"How many people?"

"What?"

"How many people will be there? At the concert?"

Dallas made a clicking sound with her tongue. "Oh, I don't know…ten thousand?"

My knees weakened as I staggered backward. This wasn't a dream at all…it was some kind of a nightmare.

"Let's get you to bed." Dallas took my arm and led me toward the staircase.

"I can't do it," I breathed. "I'm not feeling well. Tell them I can't do it. I'm not doing it."

I leaned my full weight against Dallas' lithe frame as we carefully ascended the stairs. Her body felt frail, as if I might snap her in half.

Once we made it to the top of the stairs, she spoke. "Everyone has already purchased their tickets. Backing out now would be a big problem. The label…they wouldn't like it. There would be major repercussions."

Dallas guided me into the master suite. She removed my shoes, put me into bed, and pulled the covers up to my chin.

"There you go. Get some rest. I'm calling Dr. Jones," she said, sweeping out of the room.

I listened intently as Dallas' footsteps descended the hall. Then I threw the covers off myself, scooped up my shoes, and tip-toed stealthily across the room. I spotted the top of her blonde head turning down the staircase. When she was out of view, I entered the hallway, careful to make as little noise as possible as I hurried past a series of doors. I was about to mount the first stair when a voice made me start.

"What are you doing?"

I jerked my head back. Comet was standing in his doorway.

"Nothing…just getting some water."

Comet studied me for a moment, his eyebrows scrunched and his mouth pulled into a button. “Okay.” He shrugged and disappeared back into his room.

I turned and continued my stealthy steps down the staircase. I paused at the bottom, tilting my ear toward the kitchen. I could hear Dallas speaking quietly into the phone. Careful to avoid the kitchen, I abruptly took off through the sunny foyer and then the living room toward the garage door. I threw it open and closed it quietly, pressing my back against its coldness as I attempted to slow my ragged breaths.

The lights around me clicked on, illuminating eight slots. Six of them were taken up by shiny, freshly-washed cars. I ran toward the first one, a large black SUV. Opening the door, I didn’t see what I was looking for and slammed it shut. I ran around the SUV to the next vehicle, a sleek white sedan. I repeated the same routine, again not finding what I wanted. The next car was a striking blue electric vehicle. I pulled open the driver’s side. *Bingo*. The keys sat waiting for me in the center console.

I slid hastily inside the black leather seat, tapped my destination into the navigation screen, and backed up. *Good-bye, weird world*, I thought as I escaped through the opening garage door.

Chapter Seven

Skye

I did not recognize either of the front desk clerks at The Cypress Inn when I walked through the doors. They were two thirty-something men of average height, each wearing an identical drab gray suit and a nametag. The one named Cooper had short hair that was wet with too much gel, while Riley's head was topped with a slightly unruly mop of mousy brown curls.

That I did not recognize either of them was not unusual. There must have been a stable of clerks employed here and I'd visited the hotel exactly once.

"How can I help you, Miss?" Cooper asked as I approached them. His smile revealed a mouthful of too-small teeth.

"Oh, um, I was a guest here on—" I stopped, attempting to figure out time in this alternate universe. Wasn't I actually still a guest at The Cypress? "Anyway, I need to be let into room 3A. I was recently a guest here and I think I left something."

Cooper nodded. "I see. What was it?"

"Not sure. Just a feeling. Something is missing. I really need to be the one to look."

Cooper tapped something into his keyboard. "That room is currently occupied. We will be happy to take a look for you once the current guests have checked out."

I shifted my weight from one foot to the other. "When will that be?"

Cooper pursed his lips, apparently annoyed at my prying. "Several days."

I shook my head. "No, no, no. I need to look right now. It's an emergency."

Cooper's eyes darkened. "I'm afraid that's not possible, Miss."

I sensed someone behind me, then heard a high-pitched squeal. "Skye? Skye Peters? Is that you?"

I spun around, expecting to find someone I knew. Instead, two teenage girls I didn't recognize hopped up and down behind me.

"It is! Oh my gosh. I love you. I'm your biggest fan. Can we take a picture? Please, please, please?" the red-headed girl asked.

I smiled, unsure how to act and feeling as if I were being punked.

"Sure."

I stood awkwardly as the girls squeezed onto either side of me, the smell of too-much scented body lotion hitting me. "Could you please?" the redhead said, handing her phone to Cooper.

"Oh, um…of course." Cooper straightened and aimed the phone in our direction. "Say cheese."

The girls each threw up a peace sign and leaned uncomfortably close to me.

"One more!" the blonde girl shouted as Cooper began to hand back the phone. "We have tickets to your concert tonight," she said, after Cooper had taken one more shot. "We are so psyched."

I smiled graciously. "Thank you." Unfortunately, they were going to be disappointed.

Once the girls had hurried off, I turned to Cooper expecting a fight. But his wide-eyed expression surprised me.

"I am so sorry, Miss Peters. I had no idea it was you. Please forgive me. If you'll give me just a moment, I'll get you right into that room. One moment."

Cooper ran-walked through the lobby and disappeared down a hallway.

I turned back toward the front desk. Riley had been silently watching this all go down. I glanced at him, half-expecting a request for an autograph or a photo. But he didn't say anything. He only eyed me with a slightly amused expression before returning his attention to the computer. Not a fan evidently.

Cooper returned several minutes later and escorted me up the elevator to the third floor with a frenetic kind of energy. As we approached 3A, I saw a man and a woman who looked to be in their fifties standing outside in thick white bathrobes. They were barefoot and holding wine flutes. Had they literally been kicked out of their room, naked…for me?

"Are these the occupants?" I whispered to Cooper as we approached.

"Yes," he said, as if it were the most normal thing in the world.

How humiliating.

"I am so sorry to disturb you," I said as we came to stand in front of the couple.

But neither of them looked upset. The woman's cheeks, still pink from an apparent bath, bulged as she smiled at me with adoration in her eyes. The man's expression was similar.

"Oh, no, we're happy to accommodate you, Skye," the woman said.

"Can I, um, take a photo with you?" I asked.

It felt strange and prickish to offer a photo of myself as if it were a consolation prize. But they jumped—literally—at my suggestion. The woman excitedly fumbled with her robe pockets until she found a phone.

"Would you mind?" She held out the phone to Cooper.

"I'd be happy to."

I took my place between the couple, each of them leaning in close like the teenage girls had earlier. This time, the scent of soap and cigarettes wafted up.

"I'll just be a few minutes," I said as Cooper let me into the room. Secretly, I hoped I would vanish back home. I needed to get back to Teddy.

Cooper loitered inside the hotel door as I scanned the room. It had the same four-poster bed with the engraved headboard, the same glass doors leading out to a balcony. Everything was the same, except Teddy and my things had been replaced with the unfamiliar belongings of the couple outside.

I hurried into the bathroom, the gorgeous countertops now cluttered with bottles and used washcloths. Inhaling, I pulled open the closet door and peered inside. Beyond reliving the visceral memory of being shot, and of seeing Teddy bludgeon the masked man who had shot me—it was simply a closet. I stepped inside and spun around. I looked up at the ceiling, then I placed two hands on the wall and pushed.

How the hell did I get back?

"Everything okay?" I jumped at the sound of

Cooper's voice. He had trailed me into the bathroom and was staring at me. "Did you not find what you're looking for?"

I took one more glance around and let out a deep sigh. "I'm afraid not."

"Well, we will certainly keep an eye out for you."

I exited 3A, thanked the cheerfully displaced couple once more, and headed back down to the lobby.

"We would be happy to provide you with another stay on the house, Miss Peters," Cooper offered.

"Um, okay, thanks. Maybe."

Cooper returned to the front desk as I wandered toward the entrance and stopped, milling about.

Should I take him up on his offer? Should I get a room and hide out from the impending concert?

"Pssst."

I turned at the sound of someone trying to get my attention. It was Riley, partially obscured by a large plant. He gestured for me to follow him down a side hallway. I glanced back at Cooper, who was unaware of what was happening as he typed something into his computer.

I shrugged and followed Riley. What did I have to lose, really?

He stopped at a door a few feet down the corridor and held it open for me. I paused briefly before walking inside. It appeared to be a windowless, fluorescent-lit office. The back wall was lined with boxes.

"Listen," Riley said, coming to stand across from me. He steepled his hands, glancing briefly at the floor so that his curls flopped into his eye before looking back up. "Not everyone believes the rumors about this place."

I took a step back. “What rumors?”

“That weird shit has happened. Specifically weird shit in 3A.”

My heartbeat started to race. “What weird shit?”

The corners of Riley’s mouth curved upward. He was excited to have an audience. “Sit down.” He perched on the edge of one of the desks as I took a seat in a rolling chair. “The last time something went down was back in the fifties. 1953, to be exact. There was a man and a woman who stayed in 3A. They were having some kind of clandestine affair. He was married, you see, and she was his mistress.” Riley’s eyes flashed. “Well, something went terribly awry and the man strangled her to death in the closet. Right up there.” Riley pointed at the ceiling. “The woman was pronounced dead at the scene. But that’s not where the story ends. The paramedics were able to bring her back to life.”

I interlaced my fingers tightly and leaned forward.

“She was in a coma, unconscious, for weeks,” Riley said. “And when she woke up, she was an entirely different person. She maintained that she had been alive the whole time in some kind of alternate universe. She told everyone who would listen all about it.” Riley looked up at me, darkening. “Big mistake. Of course no one believed her. She was eventually committed to a psychiatric facility and drugged up. She died there as an old woman. Quite sad, actually. But I’ve always felt strange in that room. I’ve always felt…that maybe she was telling the truth.”

I took a shaky inhale. “And why are you telling me this?”

Riley put a hand to his chin and pursed his lips,

studying me. “It was something in your eyes…like what you were looking for wasn’t physical. I don’t know, just a feeling I had.”

I looked away, his intense eye contact making me uneasy. “Well, I appreciate you telling me.”

“I’m not the only one who thought something weird went down. Teams have gone into that room, multiple teams. Looking for a portal. Because the same thing happened way back in the 1800s.”

“It did?”

“Yes. A woman who had attempted suicide by ingesting a bottle of thallium was pronounced dead. When she woke up, she said she had been somewhere else. Alive, in a separate world. But no one bought it as heaven. She shut up about it eventually, I guess, because she was allowed to live the rest of her life in peace. On a quiet farm somewhere.”

Riley peered at me.

“Something weird has happened to me too,” I said, feeling relieved to say it out loud.

He adjusted his seat on the desk excitedly and rubbed his palms together. “I knew it. Tell me. Tell me everything.”

I shrugged. “Well, basically, it’s what you just said. I was shot…I don’t know if I was pronounced dead. But now I’m living a life that’s…not mine.”

“Are you saying we’re in the alternate universe right now?”

I nodded.

Riley jumped up from the desk and clapped his hands. “Amazing.” He began pacing back and forth in the small space, coming to an abrupt stop. “You know, I’ve often wondered…if there are tasks you are supposed to complete. Like, maybe you can only come back if you hit the marks you're supposed to hit. Maybe that's the way to get back to your old life." He paused. "If you want to go back. Because those two women aren't the only people to have died in that room. They're just the only ones who have come back."

I gazed at him, mouth agape.

"Ah, you'd be pretty surprised how common that is in a hotel." He waved a hand nonchalantly.

"Okay. What am I supposed to do then?" I was aware the situation had gotten pretty grim if I was seeking advice from Riley, the slightly unstable desk clerk.

He smiled. "You live. You assume you're here for a reason and you live. What other choice do you have, really?"

"I gotta go." I stood up shakily, turning toward the door and then back again. "Thank you for telling me. I really do appreciate it."

"Of course. And don't worry." He lowered his head and winked. "Your secret's safe with me."

I smiled weakly. "Thanks."

"Seems like you got a pretty good alternate life, though. Might as well enjoy it." He held out his hand. I shook it. "Stay in touch."

I nodded, threw open the door, and headed toward the exit.

It appeared I would be singing in front of thousands of people in just a few hours. The thought of it caused a bit of breakfast to rise up in my throat threateningly.

Isn't this what I had always wanted? Thousands of paying fans lining up to hear me sing? A whole world that steps aside to let me pass? A rich and sexy husband?

Maybe this is just what getting what you want feels like: freaking terrifying.

Chapter Eight

Skye - Two years earlier

The entirety of my summer—and perhaps my entire life—had been leading up to this moment. My Northern California hometown had made me feel itchy, restless, and ready to flee for as long as I could remember. Now, I had finally done it.

When I saw the notice on social media that *Countdown to Famous*, the singing competition which had launched several famous singers, was again holding auditions, it felt like kismet. I graduated from community college the year before and had been working as a virtual assistant. It felt as if my mind had already left and only my body was present. I was clearly languishing.

When I told my mom I was moving away in one-point-five months to audition for *Countdown to Famous*, a brief sadness flickered across her features. But the look was quickly replaced by elation. She knew me better than anyone else. She knew how badly I wanted this.

The days leading up to my departure passed in a blur and, two days earlier, I had rolled into sunny, celebrity-speckled Los Angeles. As I pulled my dirt-covered Camry up to the as yet only seen online apartment complex—the sedan's interior crammed with boxes, suitcases, and a horizontal floor lamp—I was victorious. The sight of palm trees was enough to fill my chest with a bubble of enthusiasm. I didn't notice the trash-strewn parking lot or the homeless men camped out under a creased black tarp down the street. The palm trees, with their spiky, dark green leaves dancing in the balmy California wind, were enough to make me feel as if I had achieved my life's goal. I had finally made my great escape.

And yet I was far from ready to rest on my laurels. It wasn't just moving to Los Angeles that I had been dreaming of since elementary school. It was ruling Los Angeles. Being famous. Adored, lauded, applauded. I knew making it as a singer was a long shot, but I also knew it had been a passion of mine since I could talk. Why *shouldn't* wildly amazing success happen for me? If not for me, who?

I stared down at the concrete sidewalk, my black slip-ons planted a foot or so behind the lace-up boots of the woman in front of me. Beyond her, the line to audition for *Countdown to Famous* snaked alongside the massive brick auditorium and disappeared around the corner. I wasn't deterred by the thousands who also believed they had what it took to impress the judges. I still believed I had something. I was meant for something greater. I knew it.

The auditioners were a colorfully dressed mix of mostly twenty- and thirty-somethings with a few noticeably older exceptions, including a man with a long gray beard a few feet ahead. Voices rose into the air above us as people practiced their songs. A palpable nervousness radiated through the crowd.

Though the mid-morning June sun was hot, a long

narrow cover had been erected above the line to provide shade.

"Water?" A thirtysomething woman with an angled chestnut brown bob stood beside a table holding a water bottle in each hand. She was stationed just to the side of the line.

The makeshift table held plastic water bottles along with tiny cupcakes touting gaudy colored icing and tiny plastic microphones. I grabbed one of each and returned to my spot as my mind drifted to my apartment, which was still mostly empty—including my refrigerator. My plans were to purchase any requisite items after I arrived. For now I would have to sleep on a blow-up mattress, watch television on a pillow instead of a couch, and balance my laptop on a crate. It was all worth it to be in L.A. So far I had dropped off my application at a deli, a strip mall clothing store, and an insurance office. My new life was happening.

My phone pinged. It was a message from my mom.

—We're so excited for you, honey! Let us know how it goes as soon as you can!!—

"Are you nervous?"

I blinked out of my daze to find the combat-boot-clad woman ahead staring back at me. She had a creamy cocoa complexion with a hint of pink at her cheeks. Looking her over, I saw her outfit was intimidatingly stylish: a dress consisting of a rainbow-colored bandage top and a filmy, jagged-edge skirt.

I swallowed. "Not too much." Was that a lie?

"I am." The woman wrapped her arms around herself and rubbed her upper arms vigorously as if she was somehow cold in this eighty-five-degree heat. "I've never done anything like this before. I'm not even a singer, really. I'm in art school." She smiled, revealing two rows of strikingly white, straight teeth. "I just figured—what the hell? I'm Maxie, by the way. Short for Maxine."

She held out a delicate hand and I shook it. "Nice to meet you. I'm Skye. I guess my story's a bit different. Singing is what I've most loved for as long as I can remember. It's my release…my saving grace."

"Oh, wow. Well, I hope everything goes well for you, then."

"You, too."

Somehow the snaking, molasses-slow line managed to carry us around the corner, into the air-conditioned building, and finally to the side of the stage that faced the judges.

"Break a leg," I told Maxie when her turn was up. We leaned together for a quick, tight hug. Then she spun around, pressed her shoulders back, and took long strides across the stage. She stopped when she reached the duct tape X.

As she began to sing a Whitney Houston song, her voice was strong and full. She didn't seem nervous, though it was difficult to focus on her with my audition so close. The following seconds passed in a blur and then I was ushered onto the empty stage after her.

The three judges sat looking bored at a table below. The famously snarky Benny James was in the center, wearing a pinched expression. To his left was the former pop star Becki Lane, checking her phone as a makeup artist applied something to her face. To Benny's right was the skinny, sarcastic comedian Louie Topherson. How a comedian was an expert on singing I wasn't sure. But I suppose it made for better TV.

I smiled at the judges as I swallowed down the lump in my throat. It was disconcerting to suddenly see people in the flesh who you'd only seen on television. It was as if they shouldn't really exist.

I glanced to the side of the stage at the ominous black camera lens aimed at me.

"Nothing to be nervous about, darling," Benny said. "What will you be performing for us today?"

I opened my mouth to speak but was interrupted.

"Wait. First I have a question." Louie wore a smirk as he peered at me through his dark-framed glasses. "Are jean skirts still in fashion? Because I thought they went the way of visible thongs and belly chains." He snorted as Benny smiled at the insult. "Or at least they should have."

"Stop," Becki said, though she laughed too.

Humiliation bled through me as I glanced down at my denim skirt. Could this really be happening? I was being insulted before I'd even opened my mouth. My heartbeat slammed against my ribcage and echoed in my ears.

"Um…"

"And are those Payless shoes? Say it ain't so." Louie looked over at Benny with a conspiratorial grin.

"OhmyGod," Becki said, her voice a nasal whine. "Aren't you just awful today." She directed her gaze at me. "Honey, what are you singing for us?"

My face burned and I wondered if my skin was turning a shade of beet red. "They're not Payless, actually," I said, the shakiness in my voice betraying my intention to appear calm. "But there wouldn't be anything wrong with that, if they were. We can't all afford Gucci."

Louie rolled his eyes.

"My song is 'Kill 'Em With Kindness' by Selena Gomez," I said.

"Well, that's ironic," Becki said, throwing a sideways look at Louie.

"That's not how you use 'ironic'," Louie said.

Becki leaned forward to peer at Louie. "It is so," she said, jabbing one of her seven-inch pointy nails in the air.

Benny rolled his eyes and took a deep, exhausted sigh. "Proceed," he said, a deeply bored edge to his voice.

I inhaled, took a few more seconds to gather myself, and began belting out the song I had been practicing almost non-stop for the past four weeks. When I was done, I stared expectantly at the judges.

"It's a no for me," Benny said, flatly. "Next."

"C-can you tell me what you didn't like?" I said, surprising myself.

"The voice did not make up for the style," Louie said, ignoring my question.

"Sorry, honey," Becki said, wrinkling her tiny, surgically-altered nose.

I shuffled off the stage in the same surreal blur in which I had entered it. Except now there was a heavy black spot growing larger by the second in the center of my chest. It was the result of one's worst fear coming true.

I had been humiliated on national television. My most treasured passion—singing—had been beaten, stomped on, and maimed beyond recognition. Clearly I had been fooling myself all these years. It was easy to do when you were so far removed from the action, from where everything happened. I wasn't a singer. I was a joke.

"How did it go?"

Maxie was waiting for me when I stepped outside into the sunshine. Seeing her hopeful expression unleashed something within me. Tears began to pour from my eyes, and I covered my face with my hands.

"Oh, shhh," she said, enveloping me in her arms. "I'm so sorry."

I was unable to speak through my sobs for several minutes. When I finally could muster words, I only had four to say: "I'm never singing again."

Chapter Nine

Skye

"Where *were* you? I've been calling and texting for the past hour."

When I entered the house after visiting The Cypress Inn, Dallas was sitting at the kitchen table next to a woman I didn't recognize.

"I took a drive. I just needed some time to clear my head."

Dallas stood and approached me, her mouth a thin, tight line. She stopped, planting her feet across from me and folding her arms over her chest. "And did it help?"

I bit my lip, remembering Riley's face and all he had told me. "Yeah. Yeah, I think it did."

Dallas put a hand on my arm reassuringly. "Good."

The other woman came to stand beside Dallas. She was dressed in an expensive-looking beige skirt suit and a white top. Her dark, straight hair was cut bluntly around her shoulders.

"I'm so sorry to hear you've been feeling anxious again." She pulled a prescription bottle from her jacket pocket. Dr. Jones, I assumed. "I want you to take one of these each day for the next week. I believe they will help." Dr. Jones held out the bottle. I took it, glancing at the medicine name. It was long and unrecognizable. "You can take one right now. They won't make you drowsy. Then we'll see how you feel next week. I can add in something else if these don't help."

I forced a smile, having no intention of taking the pills. "Thanks."

Dr. Jones clicked her crocodile-skin heels over to the table and scooped up a coordinating crocodile-skin handbag. "I'm off. Break a leg tonight."

When she was gone, Dallas informed me we only had twenty minutes before it was time to leave for the concert. I disappeared into the bathroom, telling her I would take a pill. Instead, I shoved the bottle into the back of a drawer and leaned against the countertop taking slow inhales.

An electric current ran through my body as I anticipated performing in front of thousands of people. Yet everything felt so unreal. I couldn't be sure I would not wake up before then, my current unreal reality abruptly replaced with harsh hospital lights and the piercing *beep beep beep* of a heart monitor.

A few minutes later, Dallas knocked on the door.

"Come in," I said.

I straightened and skimmed a hand over my hair, pretending as if I had been grooming myself instead of attempting to prevent a panic attack.

Dallas stood next to me, her shoulder pressing against mine. "Even if you didn't perform the best concert ever, which is highly unlikely, you know your fans would still adore you. They love you."

She turned toward me, her eyes searching mine for signs of panic.

Her comment was reassuring. After all, it wasn't as if I was trying to impress an open-mic crowd. These people were already into me enough that they had shelled out money for a ticket.

I pressed my shoulders back and smiled. It was genuine.

"Okay. I'm ready."

****

Dallas and I approached a private entrance to the stadium where I would be performing. A thin yet muscular twenty-something man of about my height lingered at the door. He held it open to let us pass.

"Dallas said you're feeling a bit under the weather." He walked alongside us as we entered the hall of the arena. "I'm sure you'll be feeling like yourself the minute you step back onto the stage—you're such a natural. And looking amazing, as always."

I glanced at the man, feeling a bit like a prisoner on death row being escorted to their final meal.

"That's Phoenix, your choreographer," Dallas whispered.

Before I could think to respond, I found myself standing in a large dressing room, surrounded by people I didn't know. A woman began sweeping a thick, soft brush across my cheeks, as another tugged at my hair with some kind of steaming wand. A third woman began pulling off my clothes.

I stared across the room as they primped me. Ten vases overflowed with delicate white-and-yellow daisies. Their bright leaves reflected the glaring overhead lights.

"Those are beautiful," I said.

"Yes, just as you requested." Dallas stood off to the side, gazing down at a clipboard.

The woman who had undressed me now wrapped

me in a short lavender robe. She squatted at my feet, cramming them into spiky five-inch heels covered with—

"Aren't those diamonds gorgeous?" Phoenix said.

"I'm supposed to walk in these?"

Phoenix laughed, seeming to take my question as a joke.

Once the stilettos had been successfully put on, I walked in a slow line. Somehow, they felt as natural as being barefoot. I had never walked in heels as high as these—at least not for more than five minutes. Yet my body clearly seemed to disagree.

"You're going to need to do more than walk in them, doll." Phoenix winked.

I glanced up at the footage playing on a giant television mounted on the wall. It showed *me* onstage, clad in some kind of lime green, skin-tight jumpsuit. I was dancing in what appeared to be the same diamond-clad heels I was wearing.

When the strangers were finished prepping me, I wrapped my arms around myself and looked down. I was dressed in camel-toe-inducing hot pants and a bra top that pinched my skin. The outfit made the air conditioner's continual gust of air painful. I realized at that moment there was no place I would rather be less than right here, right now. I wanted comfy sweats, a couch, and a remote control—I wanted my comfort zone, stat.

My body shook as I imagined the impending performance. Even in this alternate world, I didn't want to ruin my career. I didn't want to humiliate myself by vomiting onstage or cowering in a corner in fear. That's the kind of thing that could follow you back to your old life.

Before I could voice any concerns, Phoenix grabbed my hand and pulled me down a dark, even colder hallway. We came across a group of fit men and women, stretching in tight dancewear. Each of them beamed at me, some people patting me on the shoulder and others wrapping an arm around my waist for a quick hug. These were my dancers. I watched as they formed a small circle, clasping hands and lowering their heads.

"Dear Lord," Phoenix began. "Thank you for bringing us all together and giving us this amazing opportunity to influence so many hearts and minds." I gaped at the praying group around me. "Guide us in making the right choices for ourselves, each other, and the people who seek us out for inspiration. Please be with us as we step out onto that stage tonight, be with Skye, Lord, and help us be one with your image. In Jesus' name we pray…"

The group raised their clasped hands and shouted, "Amen!"

We continued down the hallway together now. The sounds of what must be a massive crowd became audible.

"Do you hear them? They're screaming for you," Dallas whispered.

We arrived at the side of the stage, a sense of doom pervading me. I peered out as a buzzing vibrated through my limbs. There was an undulating ocean of bodies, punctuated by the bright lights of hundreds of cell phone screens. The crowd moved like an enormous beast in the dark. Sporadic shrieks echoed from different corners of the stadium.

I glanced upward. The open roof revealed a velvet blue sky punctuated with hundreds of brilliant stars. When I looked back down, a feeling of nausea overtook me.

"I can't do this," I told Phoenix. I was desperate. I considered running. But, surprisingly comfortable or not, how far would I get in these shoes?

A musical note blared from the sound system, increasing in intensity.

"It will come to you. It always does." He smiled. "Oh, and by the way. Your ex is here."

I followed the direction of Phoenix's nod across the stage. A tall, well-built man stood offstage, watching me. I squinted at him. He looked like Billie Bird, a twenty-something rapper I'd listened to in my old life.

"Break a leg." Phoenix gave me a little push onto the stage. I was half dressed and fully dazed.

Wet smoke gushed from somewhere, obscuring me from the audience. The scantily-clad dancers poured out and posed in a formation on all sides of me. A song began playing from massive speakers and lights flashed above and below, disorienting me. The intensity of the crowd's stirring increased: a hungry beast preparing to strike.

As the smoke began to clear, I was revealed to them. My gaze met that of a teenage girl standing in the front row. Her eyes bulged and her mouth fell open in a shrill scream. She held up her phone in front of her face.

The first lines of the song appeared on the teleprompter. I found myself shaking my hips and moving in time with the catchy beat, almost as if I had done this before. I was like a zombie at first—like a stiff cardboard cutout. Then something slowly began to shift. It was almost as if I knew what I was doing. Like maybe—just maybe—I was meant to do it.

The dancers moved their bodies around me at a breakneck pace. Sprays of their wet sweat hit me.

"I know you're complicated," I mouthed into a pink studded microphone. I was grateful I only had to lip sync the pre-recorded song blasting from the speakers. *"But I just can't get you off my mind. It's the way you move and the way you touch that gets me so oh-oh punch drunk."*

I swayed to the intense beat, the dancers closing in around me as the lights flashed. It was as if I was being engulfed by the music itself, as if I was being transported, pulled beneath the curtain of reality. Had I accidentally taken one of those pills after all? I felt like I was the hottest dancer in the hottest club in the world and everyone just wanted to watch me. To join me. They loved me. This was pure joy.

I stepped forward and did a little dip with my hips as I continued mouthing the words. Where had that come from? Had I just made it up or was it part of the choreography?

After the first two songs were complete, the smoke vanished. The lights ceased flashing and the dancers hustled off the stage, leaving me completely alone. Two men appeared and draped some sort of velvet cape over my shoulders. The hood of it rested on my hair as one of them clasped it at my collarbone. I had been fitted with an earpiece earlier and a voice began speaking to me. It sounded like Phoenix.

"Song three is all you. Get ready."

The slow riff of a guitar flooded the space. I moved my finger against the microphone, and it made a popping sound. It was on, live—anything I said would be broadcast clearly to everyone in the stadium.

"You can do this," the voice in my earpiece said. "Show 'em what you got."

I inhaled and sang the lyrics on the teleprompter.

At first, the sound of my naked voice was jarring. But as I continued singing, I sank into it more with every line, bringing the vocals out from someplace deep within myself.

I glanced at four girls crowded in front of the stage. Their arms were around each other as they rested their heads on one another's shoulders and swayed with the rhythm.

"We love you, Skye!"

I loved this. I felt this. Quite possibly, this very stage in this exact stadium was the only place I had ever really existed. I thought I was living before, but clearly I was wrong. This, this right here, was where I belonged. It was what I had always been looking for. It was the most comfortable place on earth. On this stage, I felt cocooned. I was safe, I was cherished, I was adored.

And I was singing. It was my own voice. It may have been enhanced every now and again, but it was my voice. Here I was living my dream. It was the dream I'd always pined for, prayed for, believed I was destined for. I now knew this world could only be a gift. There was no other option.

Each of the songs passed more fluidly than the last. The audience and I knew each other now. We loved each other. There wasn't a stranger in the stadium. We were more than friends. We were family.

As I finished my finale—another live performance—the audience erupted in shrieks and frantic applause. They didn't want me to stop. I didn't want to stop either. Yet I knew I would be back again.

I raised my hand to wave good-bye to the sea of faces, then blew them kisses. With a bow, I rushed offstage. A tangle of hands squeezed my shoulders and patted my back.

"You were amazing!"

"That was your best performance yet."

"They loved you."

I was ushered to my dressing room, which now housed an overflowing table with two metal ice buckets of Cherry Coke, carbonated water, bags of peanut M&M's, an entire cheesecake, piles of protein granola bars, a huge tray of fresh vegetables and dip, and a decadent display of heavily frosted cupcakes, chocolate *and* vanilla with sprinkles. All of my favorite foods, basically.

"See? What did I tell you?" Phoenix appeared next to me. He wrapped his arm around my shoulders. "You're a natural."

I glanced over at him, beaming so hard that my cheeks began to hurt.

"You were right."

I only had one question now. When could I do it again?

Everyone loved me here. Appreciated me. Everyone treated me like a star. My old reality suddenly felt like a foggy memory of an imperfect life. One that never quite fit.

Gazing at the snack table, I sensed Phoenix

backing away. I glanced upward and met the mischievous, brown-eyed gaze of Billie Bird. Tall and lean with a hand tucked into his trouser pocket, he was a man who clearly knew how to dress. He wore a black sweater under a teal designer suit.

"You were amazing tonight," he said.

His eyes scanned my body as he subtly licked his lips. My shoulders hunched forward. I felt like an awkward schoolgirl meeting a celebrity crush for the first time.

"Uh…thanks."

Billie took a step closer, placing one of his large hands low on my hip as he pressed his lips to my ear. He smelled amazing. "Let's get together again soon. Alone."

"Ahem. Sorry to interrupt."

Billie and I turned to find Dallas watching us, a clipboard clutched to her chest.

"Catch ya later," Billie said, winking as he strode away. I watched him go, the embodiment of swagger.

Had we…? Were we…?

Dallas aimed a disapproving look in Billie's direction before turning back to me. "Sissy Stone is here. She wants to say hi."

"Okay. Great."

A few minutes later, a large group of people drifted into the room like a mist. They came to stand next to me, parting to reveal Sissy cocooned in their center.

I watched as the pop star pulled off her sunglasses with a flourish and stepped forward in towering heels. She had a curtain of impossibly shiny blonde hair and annoyingly ample cleavage displayed in a bra top.

"So good to see you again, Skye." She leaned

forward and gave me a limp, one-armed embrace. She smelled of expensive perfume and essential oils. "You were amazing tonight."

I smiled graciously. There was little doubt in my mind at that point that I was, in fact, amazing. How many people have to say it before you believe it?

The entourage around us drifted away.

"Can we sit?" She gestured toward a leather couch pushed against the wall.

I nodded.

"I'm really trying to get where you are with my music career," she said, after we were seated. "I mean, my endorsements are enough, technically, but they're not *satisfying*. I would really love some advice."

Before I could respond, a lanky man with spiky, bleached hair and thick leather chains loped over. I studied him for a moment. It was Johnny Loss—a temperamental singer known for breaking guitars. He had multiple hits on the alternative charts.

"You know my boyfriend, Johnny." Sissy's tone was bored as she flicked a hand toward the man.

So this was who she ended up with when Mark wasn't on the table.

"Sure. Nice to see you," I said.

He jerked his head upward in response, his top lip curled. "You killed it."

I felt a rush of endorphins at the compliment from this badass musician. Before I could formulate a response, the air in my dressing room shifted and a buzz filled the room. Everyone turned to stare at the entrance.

It was Mark.

"Here's your man. We'll let you go have some

fun." Sissy stood. "But let's catch up again soon. I'll have my assistant call yours to set something up."

She teetered off on Johnny's arm, leaving me perched on the edge of the sofa.

After greeting several people with an off-putting amount of charm, Mark came to stand in front me. His towering height forced me to crane my neck.

"You ready, Freckles? The Hibiscus calls." He held out his hand to me.

"Never been more." I placed my hand in his and allowed him to pull me up. As everyone stared at us with adoration, I felt like a princess on her way to the ball.

Chapter Ten

Skye

Mark ushered me down the moonlit path to The Hibiscus. We paused in front of a small group of photographers milling around behind a velvet rope. As they excitedly clicked their cameras, we posed. I was still wearing the studded stilettos, but I had paired them with a slinky embroidered dress Dallas had helped me pick out from my vast closet earlier.

"Looking amazing, Skye!" one of the photographers shouted. "Any baby news?"

I smiled demurely, feeling surprisingly natural. After a few minutes were granted to the paparazzi, we continued toward the restaurant entrance. Mark pulled open the door for me.

Two hostesses sorting menus spotted us and transformed from cool and unbothered to jittery and nervous. The hostess with auburn hair stepped around the podium, clutching two menus.

"Mr. Campbell. Ms. Peters. So nice to see you. Please follow me."

Mark placed his hand in the small of my back as we followed her through the restaurant. She led us to a table situated on a raised podium that was shrouded by walls topped with overflowing greenery. A candle in the center of the table flickered, causing shadows to dance across the space. Beyond one wall, a pianist and a guitarist played a dreamy jazz song, their eyes closed. The setting was absolutely perfect.

Mark and I slid into the booth, and he brought his face close to mine.

"Sorry I had to miss the concert tonight, Freckles. I know you were amazing. You always are."

The low, intimate way he spoke sent a chill down my spine. And as his sparkling brown eyes peered into mine, my heart thumped wildly in my chest. Seconds seemed to morph into minutes. He finally broke the loaded silence by leaning forward and pressing his lips to my forehead.

The waiter appeared, greeting us warmly.

"Bring us a bottle of Skye's favorite Cabernet, Stuart, as well as some of those marinated olives she loves." Mark winked at me as he rested his arm on the booth behind me.

"Absolutely, sir. And I'll be right back with your French bread and olive oil."

I studied Mark as he studied the menu. Chiseled cheekbones beneath a thick shadow of sexy stubble. Dark brows and glossy dark hair. The twisted, curved muscles of his shoulders were wide enough to support a small city. And his outfit—a tailored designer suit in sleek black, with a crisp white button-down shirt. A heavy silver watch was visible beneath one cuff. All this without any input from me.

Could he be any more perfect?

Stuart reappeared within minutes, expertly pouring two glasses of thick red wine into glass goblets. The heady scent of the Cabernet wafted toward me. I fingered the glass stem as the waiter prepared our bread, holding a bottle of olive oil high as a thick stream gushed into a bowl below. A fragrant loaf of bread sat steaming in a basket nearby.

"Enjoy." Stuart gave a small nod and disappeared.

I had just tilted my head back to study the greenery behind us when I felt Mark's large hand clasp my bare knee. I instinctively jerked upward, my whole body rising briefly from the seat.

"Sorry. Didn't mean to scare you." He smiled.

I placed a hand against my heaving chest. "No, it's fine."

Mark's other hand appeared, clutching a blue box emblazoned with the golden Tiffany's logo.

"For you."

I smiled, cheeks burning. "What's the occasion?"

"No occasion needed." He moved his palm slightly higher up on my leg. "Being married to you is reason enough."

I took the box from him and flipped open the lid. I gasped. A gleaming bangle made of solid gold and encrusted with sparkling diamonds sat nestled inside the velvet interior.

"It's gorgeous."

Mark leaned forward. "So are you. Take it out."

I placed the box on the table in front of me and removed the bracelet.

"Look a little closer," he said.

I held the glimmering bangle at eye level, twisting it back and forth. Something etched inside the band caught in the restaurant's overhead lights. I brought it closer to my face.

"Read it."

I glanced at Mark, then back to the bangle. I

squinted at the scrolling letters. " 'To my moon, my stars, my Skye. Love, Mark.' "

"Here, let me put it on you."

I held out my wrist, allowing Mark to clasp the bracelet around it. The act seemed symbolic, as if it were linking us somehow.

"Perfect," he said.

Before I could think to respond, Mark leaned in and kissed me. The feeling of his lips against mine caused a surge of intense electricity to rocket through my body.

Mark pulled away and smiled at me. "All right. Let's dig in." He began using a knife to saw slices off the bread loaf as I fell back limply against the booth.

The vision of Teddy's face appeared in my mind. My chest ached. Where was he? I had been attempting to escape from him, to escape from his impending proposal, when I entered into this alternate reality. And with every passing second, I seemed to be slipping farther away from him.

Is this what I wanted?

I thought of how perfectly Mark seemed to glide through every situation, never breaking a sweat, always knowing the right thing to say. A strange realization occurred to me. I was more comfortable here, in this completely unfamiliar existence, than I ever had been in my own awkward, messy life. I was more comfortable here with Mark than I was with Teddy.

When it came to my fear of commitment, maybe there was nothing wrong with me after all. Maybe there was something wrong with *us*, with Teddy. Maybe I was simply with the wrong man.

Visions of Teddy drifted to the periphery. The

reality around me began to feel more and more as if it were actually my own.

"To my perfect wife," Mark said, raising his wine glass to me. "May we have a thousand more dinners exactly like this one."

I lifted my glass, smiling. "I couldn't have said it better myself."

Chapter Eleven

Skye

I stood in front of a green screen, twisting my hips back and forth as a large camera flashed a few feet away.

"Looking gorgeous, Skye. Just a few more," Matteo, the French photographer, called. He swept a hand over his glossy dark curls.

As I posed, a tall fan gently tousled my hair while boxy lights overhead perfected my complexion. Nearby, a rack of trendy designer outfits and a dressing table filled with more makeup than I had ever seen awaited. Three of the photographer's assistants, the makeup artist, and Dallas stood watching as I posed. It had not taken long for me to get comfortable in front of the camera. I evidently loved being the center of attention.

"Come. Look at these." Matteo waved his hand in the air and stepped out from behind the camera.

I approached a small digital screen displaying a photo he'd just snapped. It was stunning. My cheekbones cast sexy shadows on my face and my blonde hair glowed with a golden tint. Bronze body oil and heavy hair gel made it look as if I had just emerged from a mystical lagoon. I was a seductive, otherworldly creature.

And this was even before airbrushing. It was amazing what a glam squad, a world-famous photographer, and some expensive lighting could do.

"We're all done here. You were perfect." Matteo kissed his fingers and flung them into the air with a flourish. "Bless you, darling." He pulled me into a squeeze before air kissing each of my cheeks.

"How are you feeling?" Dallas appeared, holding out a cup of water as Matteo marched off with his assistants trailing.

I took a sip. "Great. That was fun."

"The next thing is your interview for the cover story. I'll tell the journalist you're ready."

A few minutes later, a brunette woman in a fitted navy tee and loose trousers followed Dallas into the studio. The woman's dark hair was slicked back into a low bun, and she wore chunky spectacles. She stopped in front of me and stuck out her hand. "Amara Rivera. I'm the writer who will be interviewing you today. Nice to meet you."

"Amara's done a ton of celebrity profiles," Dallas said.

A ruckus in the studio made us all turn. My mouth fell open as I saw Billie Bird striding confidently in my direction. He wore a long, dramatic overcoat and he was flanked by three slightly shorter men.

"What's he—"

Before Dallas could complete her sentence, Billie came to a stop directly in front of me.

"I heard you were here, baby. And damn—" He gave me a once-over. "—looking fierce as ever." He grabbed my hand and brought it to his lips. The three men behind him stared into their phones, oblivious.

"I wasn't expecting you." I looked from Dallas to Amara, then back to Billie as he let my hand drop.

"Ah, I was nearby. Thought I'd come and say hi." He leaned to the side, staring intensely at me.

"Uh-huh, that's great," Dallas said. "But Skye is kind of in the middle of something now, Billie. So I think you should…" She gave him a pointed look.

He surveyed her for a second, then nodded. "Sure…sure." He turned his gaze back to me. "But give me a call sometime soon. Okay?" He winked before turning and striding out of the studio, his trailing entourage never bothering to look up.

Amara pulled a notepad and pen from her large tote.

"I don't think we need to include that in the interview," Dallas said. "We didn't know he was coming and he's not…they're not—"

"Would you be up for having a cup of coffee at the cafe a few doors down?" Amara asked me. "We could talk privately that way."

I shrugged, still feeling the heat from Billie's kiss on my hand. "Sure."

"I'll wait for you here," Dallas said as Amara and I started toward the exit.

After a short walk, Amara and I were seated on opposite sides of a sunny booth in the corner of a retro-feeling diner. Waitresses in blue and white uniforms, striped pole accents, and ruby red booths made me feel transported to the fifties. At three on a weekday afternoon, the place was pretty much abandoned.

Amara placed her phone between us on the table. "Are you okay if I record this? It's standard practice." Her finger hovered over the screen, waiting. When I nodded, she pressed record. "You know, I really am a fan of yours so this is a thrill for me." She smiled as the steam from her cup of coffee obscured her olive complexion. "This is your third cover for Elle, correct?"

I nodded, unaware if that was actually correct or not.

"So the Sonny Awards are coming up. You are nominated for Best Pop Vocal Album, Best Solo Pop Performance, and Best Collaboration along with Billie Bird. The buzz seems to be that you're going to take them all. How does that make you feel?" Amara smiled at me.

"Amazing. It feels like a dream come true…like it's not really happening, in fact. I keep having to pinch myself."

"Well, it most certainly *is* happening. You won Best New Artist two years ago and opened the show last year—so it's not totally new to you, right? This incredible level of success?"

"Yes, that's true…but it's still hard to get used to."

"I'm sure it is. Will Mark be accompanying you to the show?"

I blinked. Would he? "Uh, yes, of course."

"I only ask because you two have sometimes avoided the red carpet. But that was mainly at the beginning of your relationship. How does it feel to be coming up on your fifth wedding anniversary?"

"Good…great. Amazing."

I could feel beads of sweat forming at my hairline. It was as if I was being quizzed on someone else's life—the life of a complete stranger. I silently cursed myself for not having Dallas fill me in beforehand.

"I assume the reason you avoided the red carpets at

the beginning of your relationship was to prevent any intrusive questioning."

"Uh, yes. Right."

"Because it was, of course, a bit of a scandal when you two first got together."

I stared blankly at Amara. "A scandal?"

She nodded slowly. "Right. Because Mark was technically married. And while he maintains that he and his ex-wife, JoJo, were in fact separated, some have disputed this claim. Including JoJo." Amara waited, watching as I swallowed a lump in my throat. "How is your relationship now? Has any of that drama followed you into the marriage?"

My cheeks burned hot. How dare this journalist pry into my private life. Even if it was a private life I had very little insight into.

"No. We have a great marriage." I lifted my chin indignantly. "It's passionate and loving. It feels like we just got together yesterday. I love Mark." I swallowed, a bit shocked at my own words.

Amara glanced down at her notepad. "That's great. You said in an earlier interview that you married Mark only two months after his divorce because, 'It just felt right. Everything about our partnership seemed natural and easy, like I'd known him forever.' "

I nodded, digesting my supposed quote. Was I actually capable of feeling that confident, that assured of a happy future?

Evidently in this life, I was.

"Yes, exactly. I guess that says it all."

"You and Billie Bird dated shortly before you got together with Mark. Your relationship lasted about two or three months, correct?"

"Okay…"

I shifted uncomfortably, the skin of my thigh adhering to the sticky booth. This woman didn't miss a beat. In fact, this was beginning to feel more like an interrogation than an interview. And I was beginning to wonder if my actions in this world would hold up to such scrutiny. I pondered whether to text Dallas. She would know how to extract me from this situation.

Amara plowed on. "Billie just made an appearance at your photoshoot. Sources say he was at your most recent concert too. Though brief, it seems the period you and Billie were together was intense. You were even engaged for a time. Is Mark comfortable with the two of you remaining such close friends?"

I was engaged before Mark? This woman truly was a wealth of information—about me.

I looked Amara squarely in the eyes and inhaled. "Yes, of course. Mark and I have total trust in each other. Billie is like a brother to me now. Our engagement was the foolish fantasy of two kids."

A warm sense of pride spread through me. I knew how to spin things. I did work in PR after all—or at least I used to.

Amara sat back against the booth, brought her coffee cup to her lips, and took a sip. It seemed her intended line of questioning was impeded. My head was buzzy and light. Blocking journalists was almost as fun as modeling for magazine covers.

"Well, it must be fun to be Skye Peters. Gorgeous, successful, wanted by the world's sexiest men—and at the top of her game, career-wise."

I shrugged, smiling demurely as I glanced into the bright sunshine just outside the window. “This life certainly has its perks.”

Chapter Twelve

Caroline - Two Years Earlier

The first day on the set of *Tunes by Teddy* held the excitement of Christmas morning as a small child. I couldn't sleep the night before, twisting in bed as nervous energy coursed through me.

When I finally met Ted the following afternoon, dopamine exploded in my veins. His brown eyes were even more mesmerizing in person, with bits of bronze and gold flakes around the stark black pupils.

"I'm Ted Sorens. Nice to meet you, Caroline." He reached out his hand to me, smiling warmly.

I could live the rest of my days hearing nothing but the sound of him saying my name. I loved the way it reverberated in his mouth, the timbre and tone of it.

"So nice to meet you, too." I slid my hand into his. A perfect fit.

During my first few months as a producer on the show, Ted recognized my work ethic. I was the first one in the office and the last one out at night. I was always the one to realize his mic wasn't plugged in or his shirt wasn't properly tucked.

I hoped he also noticed how my pixie cut had subtle blonde highlights, how I wore my shirts tucked into slim pants to show off my trim waist, and how I smelled of expensive French perfume. I hoped he noticed because I did it all for him.

Two months after our first encounter, I stood adjusting the collar on Ted's red polo shirt before showtime. Our bodies were mere inches apart. We were so close I could feel his warm breath on my face. When I glanced upwards, I found him gazing at me. My heart began pounding yet I remained calm.

Of course he was staring at me. Of course this was happening. This was always going to happen. Being together was our destiny. We could only outrun it for so long.

"Ted?" I let my hands drop from his collar.

"Yes?"

"Would you want to grab some lunch tomorrow? Maybe talk about the show? There is a Thai place I've been dying to try."

"Oh…" Ted's face reddened.

Was I too forward? Or was he just shy? No matter, he would thank me eventually.

"Sure, Caroline. Let's do that." With a taut nod, he turned and walked onto the stage. I watched, mesmerized, as he lifted his guitar from the stand, slid the thick strap around his neck, and glanced back at me with an indiscernible expression.

Ted was an amazing performer. His voice and lyrics were what had pulled me in. What had made me fall in love with him. Sure, it had been through the television screen and yes, it was a children's show. But sometimes love finds you in strange and unusual ways. It certainly had for me.

As a song began pulsating from the waist-high speakers, Ted's voice rang out. "You be nice to me, *and* I'll be nice to you, *and* he'll be nice to her, *and* they'll be nice to them *and…*" he sang. He dipped his chin and widened his eyes for emphasis in that time-honored way of keeping the attention of preschoolers.

An accidental sigh escaped from my parted lips. I wanted him so intensely. I could hardly wait until he was truly mine.

****

Upon discovering the Thai restaurant was temporarily closed the following day at lunch, Ted and I walked next door to a sunshine-filled deli. I ordered a toasted tuna salad sandwich while Ted chose the meatball sub.

"When did you start singing?" I asked, once we'd settled into a booth by the window.

Our first date. I glanced around the restaurant, cementing its features in my mind: large counter with sneeze guard, shiny gray floor tiles, the scent of bleach in the air. I flashed forward thirty years and imagined Ted and me sitting in a cozy living room recounting this very story to our grandchildren.

"Elementary school." Ted's eyes were bright with remembering. He glanced down at his tray of food and popped a kettle-cooked chip into his mouth. "I've always been into music. It's just been my thing."

"Where was elementary school?"

I knew all of this of course. *Minnesota.* I had researched and filed away these facts long before I even began looking for a job at *Tunes by Teddy*.

"Minnesota," he said. "A suburb of Minneapolis. What about you? Have you always wanted to be a producer?" He took a large bite of his sub before placing it back on the paper-lined dish and wiping his mouth with a napkin.

Of course he would ask me that. He was undeniably thoughtful.

"I'm from New Jersey, originally. But I went to college in New York and worked there for a while."

Ted nodded. "Great."

We finished the remainder of our meals in pleasant silence. Then Ted inhaled, placing his hands on the tabletop. "Should we get back?"

"Are you seeing anyone?"

Ted's eyes widened ever so slightly, a crease forming in his brow. "Uh…" He laughed nervously, pushing his plate to the side. Was he embarrassed he wasn't dating anyone? "No, I guess I'm not."

I caught his gaze, then smiled warmly, hoping to reassure him. Ted broke away from our eye contact.

"Are you free tomorrow night?" I asked.

Direct and to the point—a woman who knows what she wants. Because isn't that exactly who I was?

Ted reddened. "Uh, yeah, sure. I guess I am…"

"Wonderful." I grabbed my wallet from the corner of the booth. "There's a concert tomorrow night and a few friends and I are going. I'd love for you to join us."

Ted was silent for a moment. "Sure."

His face was unusually blank, even strained. He was probably just nervous about being alone with me. Afraid he would mess something up.

I slid my hand across the table and placed it on top of his. But he only seemed to stiffen more, waiting the appropriate few seconds before pulling away.

"You don't have to be nervous. I promise. You could never do anything wrong."

Ted looked at me strangely. Then, without a word, he slid out of the booth and walked to the cash register.

I followed. When he offered to pay for my lunch, I let him.

****

After the show the following night, Ted and I walked with my friends Cecilia and Jodi to a nearby bar. Ted opened the door for all of us.

The establishment had the dim, low-ceilinged feel of a corner bar in a tiny town, yet it was ten times larger. The space was crowded with people mingling and laughing in the smoky dimness.

Beyond the crowd in front was a sea of pool tables. The murmur of voices and music was punctuated by the occasional sound of one ball slamming into another.

After ordering drinks, Cecilia and Jodi wandered into the crowd, leaving Ted and me alone at the bar.

"What do you typically drink?" I asked.

Ted smoothed his hair from back to front, then dropped his hand to the bar top. "I'm not a big drinker. But, when I do, I usually just stick to beer."

Ted looked even cuter than usual. The polo shirt he donned for showtime had been replaced with a rust-colored plaid button-down, jeans that were the perfect combination of loose and slim, and gray sneakers. He was perfect.

Ted raised his hand to the bartender, who quickly approached.

"What do you have on tap?"

After the bartender spewed out a list of beers, Ted ordered a brown ale. Then he gestured toward me.

"And she'll have…?"

"I'll have the same."

Ted puffed out his lips and raised his eyebrows as the bartender pulled out two glasses from below the bar.

"You're a beer fan as well?" he asked.

Ted looked at me longer than he had ever had before. I silently praised myself. Going along with what a man liked was as old as the Bible itself.

"I don't hate it," I said.

I smiled and batted my eyelashes as the bartender set two cocktail napkins on the bar and placed our drinks atop them. Ted raised his glass into the air.

"To many more successful shows together," he said, smiling.

I swallowed. It wasn't the toast I had been hoping for. The toast I had been hoping for was something more along the lines of *"Here's to whatever the night brings."*

No bother. I wouldn't let that stop me. I pulled up the corners of my mouth into a smile and clinked my glass against Ted's.

After knocking back his first beer, Ted slid out a barstool, propped a leg on the bottom rung, and sat down. So we were getting comfortable. This was good. I did the same.

"I'll have one more of those," Ted called out to the bartender.

"Two," I corrected, downing the last swig of my beer and placing the stein back down on the bar. Ted glanced over, letting his eyes linger in mine.

"You definitely don't have a beer gut. I'm impressed by how fast you drank that."

Ted's eyes flicked down to my stomach, and I instinctively smoothed my hand over the area.

I would never wear a dress. Still, I had upgraded from my normal work look. My typical button-down had been replaced with a stretchy viscose top and my work slacks were swapped out for tight black jeans. For the first time since I'd met him, I felt as if Ted was noticing me—noticing my body. It wasn't as if I was looking for a cheap thrill so I was fine with the slow pace. I wanted Ted to get to know the whole me—mind, body, and soul.

Halfway through our second beers, I decided to take a chance. I put my hand midway up Ted's thigh. He froze, his beer hovering somewhere between the bartop and his mouth. Finally, he set his beer down.

"I'm sorry if I've led you on, Caroline. But I'm not looking for…a relationship."

I smiled serenely. "Me either."

Ted narrowed his eyes. Eventually, he picked up his beer and took a long swig.

Though I wanted to move my hand a few inches higher on his thigh, I pulled it away. *Be patient, Caroline. All in good time.*

I returned my empty beer stein to its wrinkled napkin, and I held up my finger to the bartender.

"Two shots of Jäger, please."

Ted leaned forward, laughing stiffly. "What? Whoa now, I don't know…"

Cecilia and Jodi appeared beside us with two strange men at their elbows.

"Are we doing shots?" Cecilia exclaimed, throwing a hand into the air. "All right!"

The group crowded around us.

"Make that six shots." Cecilia slid a credit card out of her jeans pocket and pressed it to the bar.

Almost instantaneously, a tray of six shots materialized before us. The glasses were so full that some sloshed out as the bartender slid them over.

“Enjoy,” he said.

Everyone eagerly grabbed their shot—all except Ted. He hesitated for a moment. But then he shrugged as if to say, “What the hell?”

I imbibed the liquid in one quick swallow, feeling the heat of it slide down my throat and into my chest like a flame. As I set the shot glass back on the bar, Ted and I locked eyes for one loaded second. Something heavy hung between us. I reached forward and grabbed his warm neck with both of my hands, pulling him toward me. I pressed my mouth against his, sliding my tongue between his parted lips. He was stiff at first—and not in the way I wanted. His body was rigid and his hands hung limply at each side. He mumbled a resistant “Caroline” into my mouth but I didn’t stop. I refused to stop.

Finally, as if the alcohol had just hit his bloodstream, his shoulders softened against me and his arms slid around my waist.

“Woo hoo!” someone whooped in the background.

Ted and I continued kissing like that for several seconds as my friends drifted back into the crowd. When we finally pulled apart, Ted wouldn’t look at me. I waited for him to say something—anything—but he didn’t.

The smallest sliver of irritation created a twinge in my chest. I was willing to work for Ted, but *damn* was he making it difficult. I knew I was attractive, plus we were both available—and drunk. At this point, the only thing Ted had to commit to was one night with me and he still seemed hesitant.

“So?” I said, finally breaking the uncomfortable silence. Ted glanced sideways at me. “Wanna go to my apartment?"

As Ted parted his lips to respond, a woman who seemed to materialize from space slammed into him. She had white-blonde hair that just grazed her shoulders, tacky peach-colored lip gloss, and a slim, hourglass shape. Her half-empty beer sloshed down the front of his shirt.

"Excuse me." I attempted to fling the woman back into the crowd.

But something was happening between Ted and her. She had fallen directly into his arms and it was as if they were frozen like that. They stared into each other's eyes, making me feel suddenly like an intruder—an interloper.

What the hell was happening here? Just seconds ago, Ted and I had been engaged in a passionate kiss.

"Oh, gosh, I'm so sorry," the woman said. Ted finally removed his arms from around her, but not his gaze.

A striking Black woman appeared, her skin dewy with perspiration. "We were dancing and I spun her right into you." She raised her hand to her mouth, laughing.

I scowled at them. This was so not funny.

"It's no problem. I'm Ted, by the way." He reached out to shake the blonde's hand, then her friend's.

"Skye," the blonde said.

"Maxie," said the friend.

"Oh, wait, what—you don't recognize me?" Skye said. Her forehead was sweaty and one of the straps from her tank top dangled off of a bare shoulder.

Ted's smile was brilliantly wide. He hadn't

glanced at me even once since the woman had appeared. "No, I guess not. Should I?"

"I just embarrassed myself in front of the whole world—live, on national television." She stumbled sideways, taking the last remaining swig of her beer.

"You didn't embarrass yourself," Maxie said. Her tone was gentle, reassuring. "That judge was a total jerk. You did fine…"

The blonde scoffed.

"I was on *Countdown to Famous*," she said. "And—I blew it." She abruptly burst into tears, holding up the beer bottle to shield her face.

Her friend put an arm around her protectively. "You're going to be fine, sweetie."

Ted's smile vanished. He appeared genuinely concerned for this stranger. In fact, he expressed more emotion *for her* than he ever had *for me*—the woman he was meant to be with. "Will you give me a chance to cheer you up then?" he said.

The woman wiped her wet cheek with the back of her hand and glanced up at Ted, one eyebrow cocked flirtatiously. "Maybe."

"First you have to tell me your last name," he said.

The pair locked eyes. In the heat of their intensity, I once again felt as if I was intruding.

"Sure." The woman was no longer crying. "It's Peters."

"Okay, Miss Peters, I'm going to teach you a really cool dance move. Come with me." He wrapped his arm lightly around Skye's waist and led her into the crowd. When Maxie and I were alone, she raised her eyebrows at me before wandering away. I continued to observe the pair through an opening in the crowd. Ted demonstrated a ridiculous dance move, kicking his leg off to the side. Skye attempted to mirror the move as she stood close to him, the crowd on the dance floor pushing them even closer together. She leaned into him, laughing. Then the crowd between us abruptly closed in.

I left the bar shortly afterward without waiting for Ted to return. I was making a point. He couldn't do whatever he wanted and expect me to be there waiting for him.

****

Two weeks after the bar incident, I still had no idea whether Ted had seen the blonde woman again. But what I did know is that he barely looked at me. So one afternoon as the makeup artist powdered Ted's nose, I approached him.

"That woman you ran into at the bar was adorable." I placed a hand lightly on his arm.

"Skye? Oh, yeah…" He sounded as if he thought I was full of it—or rather *knew* I was full of it. No issues there. I wouldn't expect any less from the man I was going to marry.

"So are you going to see her again?" I asked.

Ted turned his head to look at me, sizing me up. "Yes. I *have* seen her again."

My heartbeat faltered in spite of my complete confidence in the future. Our future. "Great."

"I really like her. She's just—she's different, you know?"

I almost vomited that morning's toast and oatmeal. Different? This woman had really done a number on him. Still, I wasn't going to miss the opportunity to find out as much as possible.

"How many dates have you been on?"

"Two."

Blood rushed to my cheeks as my heart jackhammered in my chest. What was it about this ridiculous woman? She was obviously some phase Ted needed to go through.

"I'm so happy for you." I barely managed a smile before walking away.

This was not how any of this was supposed to go—me falling in love with Ted via his television show, me searching for jobs on his show for over a year, me uprooting my entire life to relocate to the West Coast.

Was Skye some kind of a test? Was she some irritation, a gnawing pebble in my shoe, something I just had to endure?

I didn't believe in passivity. If this awful woman was standing in the way of me and my destiny, I would need to take action. She would need to be removed.

Little did I know just how persistent of an irritation she would be.

Chapter Thirteen

April 2nd, Three a.m., Two Years Earlier

Ted: —*Hey, u awake?*—

Aiden: —*Ted? Wrong number. This ain't your booty call.*—

Ted: —*I think I met my future wife.*—

Aiden: —*WTF? What time is it?*—

Ted: —*Yess*—

Aiden: —*Little bro, I got kids. And I'm 2 hours ahead of u. I'll be awake in an hour.*—

Ted: —*She is incredible, man.*—

Aiden: —*Where'd you meet this incredible LA woman?*—

Ted: —*A bar.*—

Aiden: —*Classy.*—

Ted: —*She's from Northern California, some small town.*—

Aiden: —*What?*—

Ted: —*She's gorgeous*—

Aiden: —*LA face with an Oakland booty?*—

Ted: —*She's funny*—

Ted: —*She's blonde*—

Aiden: —*I'm calling you in an hour when the kids wake me up.*—

Ted: —*Her name is Skye.*—

Ted: —*With an E.*—

Aiden: —*Text me when you schedule the wedding. Night, bro.*—

Chapter Fourteen

Skye

I had no idea how uncomfortable the seats at the Shrine Auditorium were. Their plasticky top edge dug into the exposed skin of my back while the thinning cushion made my ass ache. Nonetheless, the chair's discomfort didn't detract from the absolute dreamlike experience of being at the Sonny Awards. *Of being nominated for a Sonny award.* I had grown up watching them every year, lip-syncing my favorite songs into the mirror during commercial breaks. Now I was here—as a nominated singer and a performer, no less.

I shifted in my third-row seat, uncrossing and recrossing my legs under the shimmering full skirt of my golden Dolce & Gabbana gown. Mark, smelling of intoxicatingly expensive cologne and looking perfect in a tailored Armani suit, rested his hand in my lap. He had escorted me down the red carpet with his palm in the small of my back, then into the dome-like auditorium. Icons I had grown up watching on television—Mariah Carey and Celine Dion, for starters—had greeted me as old friends do, pressing their warm cheeks against mine and smiling widely at me. It was surreal.

A twenty-something man with a bulky camera on his shoulder crouched in the aisle a few feet away, aiming the lens at me. I hardly recognized myself as my image was broadcast onto the huge screen next to the stage. After hours of fawning and prepping, my hair had been swept into a bejeweled knot, my nails had been painted to coordinate with my gold glittering bodice, and my entire body had been sprayed with a subtle fake tan. I pushed the corners of my mouth into a smile.

"And the award for Best Collaboration goes to…"

The auditorium fell silent as a rapper with honeyed skin and enormous fake breasts peeled open a white envelope on stage. She glanced at the card inside and then looked up, smiling. "Skye Peters and Billie Bird for their song, 'Achin' for Another Chance'." The audience erupted into applause before she could finish reading the card.

An electric buzz flooded my senses. People in front of and beside me turned to stare and clap, including several familiar famous faces.

"You did it, Freckles. Congratulations." Mark pressed his mouth into my ear.

We both stood and I turned to embrace him. Then I lifted the full skirt of my dress slightly and took a step forward in my clear platform pumps. A few seconds later, Billie appeared from somewhere deeper in the auditorium. He took my hand and led me up the few stairs to the stage. Several men and a woman I didn't recognize, likely producers or co-writers, gathered around us at the podium.

The buxom presenter congratulated us as she handed Billie and me a Sonny statue. The metal award was heavy and cold in my grasp.

"Thank you so much for this award," I said into the

mic, the closeness of my mouth causing a bit of feedback. I stared into the faces in the front rows, quickly locating Mark's. "I have dreamt of becoming a singer since I could talk. Getting to this point in my career…it's truly a fantasy. Being given the award alongside so many greats in the industry—" I scanned the famous faces, all peering up at me. "—it's surreal."

I stepped to the side, allowing Billie to approach the mic. He did so, then turned back and waved the Sonny Award at me. "First and foremost, I'd like to thank Skye Peters. Without her talent and passion, none of this would have been possible." He winked at me, then completed the rest of his speech.

The group of us were escorted backstage, where we were instructed to stand in front of a small collection of seated reporters. The rest of the group fell behind Billie and me.

"Congratulations," a man with a lanyard around his neck said. "How was it, writing and performing this song together?"

I glanced up, wide-eyed, at Billie, his lanky frame towering over me. I had no recollection of either writing or performing with Billie. Luckily, he flashed a mischievous half-smile to the reporters.

"I think that might have been the best part of this whole thing…spending time with this woman right here."

The press laughed.

"It wasn't weird?" a red-headed woman asked. "With your history, and Skye being married now?"

Billie shifted his weight. "I'll take what I can get."

I cleared my throat and moved closer to the mic, feeling as if I should defend my honor. "Of course we are only friends. Absolutely nothing happened between us, let me make that clear. But, yes, it's been great seeing Billie again."

A third reporter held up his phone, using it as a recorder. "And, Billie, what do you say to the rumor that at least one of the songs on your upcoming album was written specifically to Skye's husband, Mark Campbell? A diss track?"

Billie shrugged, his smile fading. "People can say what they wanna say. I write the songs. It's not my job to tell y'all what to think about them."

A spattering of whispers danced through the space.

"Skye, you and Mark just celebrated your fifth wedding anniversary," the red-headed reporter said. "Can we expect some baby news anytime soon?"

My cheeks burned as I forced a smile. Having a baby with Mark was unfathomable. It would mean having sex him, after all, and, in my heart, I was still very much connected to Teddy.

"No news yet. We'll keep you posted."

After several more questions, we were released back to our seats. As I was about to step out of the backstage area into the auditorium, I felt an arm slide around my waist. I turned just as Billie leaned down to press his mouth against my cheek.

"Let me know when you're free sometime. I'd love to have a drink with you and…you know, catch up. Like old times."

The wetness of his mouth caused a chill down my spine. It was gross. I pulled away. "Sure. I'll let you know."

I turned away from his leering gaze and was just about to return to my seat, when a woman in a headset grabbed my arm.

"Ms. Peters, you're needed in wardrobe. Your performance is coming up."

My mouth fell open. My performance? "Oh. Okay…"

My stomach flip-flopped slightly at the thought of performing in front of celebrities I had grown up watching. But I felt confident that whatever came out of my mouth would sound pretty damn good. All of the experience I had gained in my forgotten past had paid off at my concert. It would pay off here too.

I trailed the woman to a separate backstage area. Two other women I didn't recognize began undressing me. My full-skirted gown with the shimmering bodice was replaced with a shiny sequin dress that barely covered my ass. Headset Lady then escorted me back to the edge of the stage and told me exactly when to step onto it.

"You're up."

I strutted up to the mic, frantic fans at the back of the auditorium screaming and shouting my name.

"Skye! We love you!"

The live band on stage behind me began strumming and stroking out the notes from a familiar slow song. I gazed forward as the lyrics flashed onto the teleprompter. Then I went for it. I opened my mouth and belted out the words, aware of a sea of famous faces staring at me.

First I met the gaze of Billie, who winked lecherously, then I spotted Mark. His hands were steepled in front of his mouth and his gaze was intense. He seemed to be hanging on my every word. He was nervous for me, I realized—for this big, televised moment. It was sweet.

When the song ended, a hollowness filled my belly. I was reluctant to leave the stage. I didn't want this surreal moment to end. I let my hand holding the mic fall to my side as the audience erupted into applause. I slid one leg behind the other and bowed like I was greeting the queen. I could definitely get used to this. I *was* getting used to this. The stage was my second home.

After accepting their adoration, I strutted away to find the woman in the headset waiting for me off-stage. She gushed about how incredible I was before leading me back to the same two women who then undressed and re-dressed me in my earlier golden gown.

Finally, I took my seat next to Mark.

"You were amazing," he said, placing his hand in my lap. "They're just about to announce Best Solo Pop Performance."

Minutes later I was back onstage, accepting my second award of the night. A half-hour later, I also took the grand finale award—Best Pop Album of the Year.

As I stood at the podium giving my third acceptance speech, it felt as if I had spent more time on stage than in my actual seat. Evidently the comfort of the chairs was immaterial. The stage was my domain. The audience was *my* audience—we were intimately acquainted now.

"This means the world to me." I held the Best Pop Album award up with both hands. Unexpectedly, tears began sliding down my cheeks. "I never dared to dream this big. Never dared to believe my small, persistent inner voice, the one urging me to sing, the one telling me to listen to my inner calling. I never imagined following it would lead me here." I paused, the audience rapt as they awaited my next uttering. "Listen to it, people. Follow that voice."

The crowd exploded into applause.

Chapter Fifteen

Skye

After the awards show, Mark and I headed to the Vanity Fair afterparty. As we made our way through the darkened space, a few people I recognized and a lot of those I didn't came up to offer their congratulations.

I had won all three awards. I was the person to be. I was the belle of the ball.

"I finally got you alone," Mark said.

Our bodies were pressed close together in a private booth, his arm resting behind me. A waitress working the room delivered our drink orders—a beer for Mark, a Cosmopolitan for me. I fingered the stem of my glass as I gazed up at him through my lashes. When Mark put his attention on you, it was intense.

"Was that your goal?" A coy smile played at the corners of my lips.

"Always."

He grinned a devastating half-smile that made his dark eyes sparkle while drawing my attention to the thick stubble around his mouth. God, he was good-looking.

I was currently in my third outfit change of the night: a short, slinky, navy number with thin straps. Mark had tossed the jacket of his tux into the seat beside us, his bowtie undone. The top two buttons of his white shirt were opened, revealing a hint of bare chest. He abruptly reached across himself to clutch my exposed thigh with his palm.

"Let's make a baby, Peters." His voice was a low growl as his lips grazed my ear.

I pulled away to look at him, my heartbeat jackhammering in my ribcage. "Are the reporters getting to you?"

Mark sat back, removing his hand from my thigh and looking away in thought. I exhaled quietly, secretly relieved to have a little space between us.

"No." He looked pointedly at me. "It's just a good time. You've achieved all your career goals. The public can afford to do without you for a little while. Your career will survive. It's my turn."

He leaned toward me, his mouth inching ever closer to my own as he gazed at me with a dreamy look in his eyes. He seemed to really want me. To love me. It was intoxicating.

"*Ahhh*, can you believe it? You won *them all!*"

A male voice caused both of us to turn. Phoenix was scooting into the booth across from us. His mouth fell open as he stared forward, blinking. "Oh, no. Sorry to interrupt."

Mark inhaled, glancing at me then back at Phoenix. "No, it's not a problem. I need to be heading out anyway."

I looked over at him. "You're leaving?"

"Yes. I've got meetings in New York tomorrow. I'm taking the red eye. Remember?"

As he reached over to grab his suit jacket, the flex in his bicep was evident beneath the thin material of his shirt. Phoenix and I both gaped.

"Bye, Freckles." Mark stood. "I'll call you tomorrow. Have fun." He leaned down, gave me a quick peck on the cheek, and winked. Phoenix and I watched as he strolled away.

"Your husband is dreamy."

My cheeks burned, but I couldn't formulate a response. I felt like a hormonal teenager with a crush. I needed a fan. I was practically overheating.

"Dreamy or not, he abandoned me. So I'm lucky you're here. Ready to celebrate?" I flashed Phoenix a smile.

"Oh, actually, I have to go too, doll." He nodded toward the bar. I followed his gaze to a sharp-looking, ginger-haired man in a printed shirt. "Easton and I are celebrating our anniversary tonight and I promised him a little *alone time*." He slid out of the booth and walked over to my side. "I'm so proud of you, lady. I'll see you next week." He leaned down, kissed me lightly on both cheeks, and headed into the crowd.

I stared blankly down at the phone in my lap. Dallas had to unexpectedly fly home to (where else?) Dallas a few days earlier for her mom's unplanned appendectomy. If she was here, she most certainly would be celebrating with me. But she wasn't…

I scooted out of the booth, my half-drained Cosmo in one hand, and glanced around. Small groups of people stood chatting or laughing. I saw Billie, now wearing a white cashmere turtleneck beneath a black blazer, staring directly at me. I looked away, my eye landing on a small, white-blonde head bowed in the back booth. I squinted. It was Sissy Stone. She wore a square-neck mini-dress, her full D-cups practically touching her chin. Two women I didn't recognize sat in the U-shaped booth next to her, staring at their phones. I headed toward them, stopping at the end of their booth.

"Hi, Sissy."

"Oh my God, Skye." Sissy scooted down and patted the space beside her. "Join us. You were so incredible tonight. And winning all those awards…wow. You *so* deserve them."

As I squeezed in beside her, I noticed her breath wreaked of pungent alcohol and her pupils were large and unfocused.

"Sorry if I seem distracted, by the way," she continued. "I'm sure you've heard the news."

I stared blankly at her. "The news?"

"Oh. Well, let me fill you in. Johnny cheated on me with two strippers. TMZ has it all on film—he had sex with them in the VIP room. *Both* of them."

I made a face, the sordid vision making me want to expel my Cosmo. "Oh my God. That's awful…I'm so sorry." I laid my hand lightly on her shoulder. "Are you okay?"

She shrugged, her lips pouty. "Well, it wouldn't be so bad if I wasn't in love with him, y'know?" Her phone lit up on the table in front of her. "Shit, that's him."

The two women at the table glanced up. "What's he saying?" one of them asked.

Sissy's face melted into a soft smile. "He wants to see me."

"Awww," the women said.

Sissy began scooting in my direction. "Sorry. I gotta go."

I slid back out to let her pass. As she stood, it

became obvious her skintight dress had inched upward, exposing a bit of her green lace panties. She tugged the dress down, stumbling slightly in her platform shoes. Slurring, she said, "The heart—it wants what it wants."

She shrugged at me again, then headed toward the exit with her two mostly mute friends in tow.

I took that as my cue to leave. When I was alone in the car, unencumbered by the usual supervision of Mark and Dallas, an urge overtook me. I leaned forward in my plush leather seat toward the driver.

"Before heading home, I want to make a stop."

The town car pulled up in front of Teddy's ranch-style house a half-hour later. Even in the dark, I could see its familiar facade. The thinning grass of the front yard led to a row of flat-top shrubbery growing snugly against its front. A long, narrow roof covered the front porch, which now housed a circular table and two chairs. Deep red bricks were accented with freshly painted black shutters.

"Give me fifteen minutes," I said, slipping out of the car.

Heels in hand, I tip-toed stealthily through the darkened yard and around the side of the house to a window shrouded from the street by a small wall. This was where the office should be. I peered through an opening in the curtains, expecting to see Teddy's guitar hanging on the wall.

My first sign something was off were the drapes. They were new. Before, there had been only blinds. I took in the space. Almost instantly, my heartbeat increased and my breathing became rapid. In the gentle illumination of a bubbling night light I saw a wooden crib pushed up against a wall. A pastel quilt was displayed above it. In the corner was a rocking chair, with a changing table opposite it.

Was this the right house? I had verified that the address was still attached to Teddy's name before the trip. This had to be correct. But none of this made sense. Teddy? A baby?

I tip-toed toward the back of the house, dirt clinging to the soles of my bare feet. I rounded the corner into the backyard and halted beside a tall shrub. From there, I could see into the glass patio doors leading from the living room into the backyard. I peered inside.

A flickering television illuminated something odd-shaped on the couch. As I stared, the shape began to take form. Two people were huddled beneath a blanket. A woman's head rested on the shoulder of a man, her eyes closed. She was asleep. The man gazed at the television. I studied the curve of his shoulders, the way his thick hair stood up a little, the reflection of light in his brown eyes. It was Teddy. It *was* his house. And he wasn't alone.

In this version of reality, Teddy had a different partner—presumably a wife and at least one child.

It all made sense, really. This was what he had always wanted—what I was denying him.

I watched him for a beat longer before turning and running back along the side of the house. I was just about to head toward the road when the sound of crying made me stop. I crept back over to the side window and peered inside. Teddy appeared in the doorway of the now-nursery, hastily crossing the room and scooping up a small infant into his arms. I watched as he placed the child on his shoulder and began to pace back and forth, patting the child's back.

How had I never envisioned what Teddy would look like with a baby before? How had I never imagined what it might do to me? He looked so natural. So right. I became aware of something warm and gooey at my center. It had the doughy, chocolatey consistency of a chocolate chip cookie just pulled from the oven.

Teddy paused in front of the crib, his back to me as he swayed in the moonlight. In the gentle glow, I could just make out the lines of sinewy arms and the outline of his butt beneath a pair of gray knit shorts. As I studied him comforting his child, a thought occurred to me: She's lucky. Whoever the person dozing on the couch is, she is a lucky woman. I want to be her.

A stabbing pain abruptly pierced my heart. Quite possibly, it was too late for all of that. Quite possibly, I would never get my chance to try for a life like this with Teddy. And maybe that's what I deserved. Feeling like an outsider to Teddy's life was painful. It was something I never wanted to feel again. I forced my gaze away, crept back through the front yard, and slipped into the waiting car. Everything suddenly felt heavy and dark.

"Take me home, please." I glanced once more at Teddy's house before swiftly looking away.

****

I drifted in and out of sleep on the way home, awakening as we pulled up to the heavy iron gate in front of the house. As my eyes came into focus, I saw an olive-green Range Rover I didn't recognize parked outside. We pulled up next to it. The blackened driver's side window rolled down and Billie's face appeared. He wore a wolfish grin.

I briefly considered ignoring him and rolling through the gate without another word. But for some reason I rolled down my window.

"Yes?"

"Hey, Skye. Can I come in?"

"Um…what are you doing here?"

He shrugged. "I figured you'd be alone and…I wanted to keep you company. You know, make sure you're not lonely."

I eyed him for a beat, then gave a quick nod. His grin widened. After the pain of seeing Teddy with a family, I didn't want to be alone.

I slid across the seat and scanned my ID into the control panel. The gate opened and the driver pulled up to the front of the house. I slipped out of the car as Billie parked behind us.

"Goodnight," I said as the driver pulled away.

I tapped the security code into the front door panel, not looking back but feeling Billie's presence behind me. I stepped inside the tiled foyer and Billie followed, closing the door behind him. The entire house was dark except for the moonlight shining through the windows.

Billie wore a heavy gold-and-silver chain which rested against his white cashmere sweater. His thick, brown curls were wet with some kind of gel.

"Thanks for letting me come in," he said, his voice soft as he rubbed his palms together and licked his lips.

I dropped my shoes onto the tile floor with a loud thud.

"Yeah, I—"

Before I could finish, Billie pressed me up against the wall. As his groin pinned me there, he inserted his tongue between my parted lips.

Shocked, I shoved him away hard. He looked at me guiltily.

"No!" I shouted. "That won't be happening. I'm married so, just…no."

Billie was silent for a moment as we gazed at each other. I waited for him to argue or plead his case—to tell me he was in love with me. Instead, he just shrugged, said "okay," and strode into the living room.

"Lexi, turn on the living room lights," he called into the darkness.

Light flooded the room. How did he know? I trailed behind him, staring as he plopped down on my couch with his legs spread wide apart.

"Can you grab me the remote, baby?" he said.

Confused, I hesitated for a moment. Then I lifted the remote from the shelf next to the television and handed it to him.

"And maybe some snacks?" He aimed the remote at the television.

I peered at him, wide-eyed. "Huh?" Was this guy serious?

As I took a step unsurely toward the kitchen, Billie slapped me hard on the ass. "Thanks, baby."

My butt stinging, I walked into the massive pantry and stood there for several minutes, catching my breath. Finally, I rifled through the items and pulled out an unopened bag of barbecue potato chips. I carried it back to him, the television now flashing a football game. As I moved around the couch, my eye caught on something on Billie's phone screen. He was video-chatting with someone. I blinked, my breath catching as my eyes focused. A pair of large, slightly asymmetrical breasts filled the screen.

"Do you like what you see, Billie?" a female voice breathed.

My mouth fell open.

"I do, baby. I do. Send me some stills. A few different angles."

"What the hell? Get out!" I shouted, throwing the chip bag on the couch.

"Gotta go, baby." Billie ended the call and glanced up at me. "What? I can't stay a bit longer?"

I narrowed my eyes at him, gritting my teeth. "I'm pretty tired."

Billie shrugged and stood up. "Sure."

I followed him through the house to the front door and onto the small porch. Arms crossed over my chest, I waited for him to descend the stairs. Instead, he turned, grabbed me roughly by the shoulders, and pressed his mouth hard against my own. Again, his slithery tongue slid between my lips.

"Ew, *get off,*" I said into his mouth.

I tried to shrug out of his grip, but he didn't let me go for several seconds. It was so easy for him, holding me against my will. I was powerless. If he wanted to assault me right there, he could. A few seconds later, he released me and strode away. When he reached the driver's side door of the SUV, he looked back.

"Thanks, baby," he said, winking. "I owe you one."

I stood for a moment, contemplating why exactly he owed me as he navigated his SUV out of the driveway, bass thumping loudly. As his taillights sped into the darkness, I realized something. Every time I heard a Billie Bird song, I would remember the sour taste of his breath and the shitty way he made me feel.

I walked back inside, slammed the door shut, and locked it.

Chapter Sixteen

Skye

When I opened my eyes Monday morning, I went from early morning zen to middle-of-the-day tense in a millisecond. Someone was sitting at the edge of my bed.

“Dallas? What are you doing here?”

As accustomed as I was to having assistants surrounding me at all times, someone watching me while I slept was a bit too close even for me. I struggled to sit up as Dallas turned to look at me. She pushed a phone into my face.

“*This*. I’m here about *this*.”

I squinted at the image on the screen. Two people, a bit blurry and from a distance. Why should I care about this?

Then I saw the sparkly dress and the white cashmere sweater. It was a photo of Billie and me from two nights earlier. We appeared to be kissing on the front porch.

“Did this really happen?” Dallas shook her head, squeezing her eyes shut. “No, that’s none of my business. *How* did this happen? How did you give them the opportunity for this shot?”

“Nothing happened.” I sat up, the comforter and sheets pooling around my waist. “Billie showed up at my house after the Sonny's afterparty and I let him in. I kicked him out about ten minutes later—but he forced himself on me outside, on the porch. After I'd already told him no once inside."

Dallas's jaw was set in a tight line. "He must have tipped them off." She held the phone in the air, waving it as she spoke. "This was taken after two a.m. He must have tipped the paps off and they were waiting outside the gate."

I struggled to comprehend this. Tipped off the press?

But the more I considered it, the more it made sense. *That* was why he kissed me outside a second time. *That* was why he held onto my shoulders and refused to release me. It was all to make sure the photographers he set up could get their shot.

"That asshole…but why would he…?"

"Press for his new album, of course." Dallas was matter-of-fact. "This doesn't shine a good light on you. A cheating wife is not the image we're going for. Some of your fans will be pissed—and it will be your word against his. It's just a matter of whoever's team can do the best spin of these photos." She inhaled as if she were exhausted. "And that's just professionally. There's also your personal life…"

As if on cue, the phone on the comforter beside me began buzzing. It was Mark.

"I'll give you some privacy."

Dallas left the room as I scooped up the phone and slid out of bed.

"Skye? What's going on? What the hell happened?"

It was rare that Mark used my actual name. It

sounded almost like a bad word coming from him. I didn't like it.

"Absolutely nothing happened."

Though I felt as if I was playing a part in this new world, I would play it. Defending myself against Billie, someone who was trying to screw me both literally and figuratively, was purely instinctual.

"Billie showed up at the house last night and he forced himself on me. Twice. He kissed me—but nothing happened. I told him to get out. He's a liar. He used me. He tipped off the press—he had to have."

Mark was silent. As I waited, I padded back and forth in front of our double sink vanity, inside of my closet, then his. There among his things, *our* things, I began to consider a life with him. We did seem to work together. And Teddy was married. I fingered a bottle of cologne sitting on a shelf in Mark's closet.

I sensed an aura of calm coming from the other end of line. Finally, he took a slow breath. "It's okay, Freckles. We'll figure this out."

At the sound of his nickname for me, I released the breath I had been holding. It felt so good to hear him say it.

"Thank you. Thank you for believing me."

"Listen, I gotta go. We'll talk more about this tonight. Bye."

****

Dallas was on the phone most of the morning, fielding questions about the photos and discussing a damage control game plan with Francesca.

"You remember you've got that movie premiere tonight, correct? The new Sofia Coppola film?" Dallas reminded me of this a few hours after I'd spoken to

Mark. “The Galvan Dress is hanging outside your bathroom door. Take the metallic Stella clutch with it. Your team will be here at four.”

“My team?”

“Brenda and Leslie—your glam squad?”

“Oh, of course…” I tried to play off my cluelessness, but Dallas didn’t appear to buy it. “Is Mark going?”

“Yes. His flight should be arriving in a few hours.” She paused. “It’s actually great timing. You two can show everyone that picture of you and Billie is absolute bullshit—that you are as happy and strong as ever.” She forced the corners of her mouth into a smile before jabbing a finger onto the phone screen and bringing it to her ear once again.

My glam squad arrived right on time. The effervescent Brenda gracefully sidestepped any Billie talk, instead talking about her gaming-obsessed boyfriend as she smeared, buffed, and dotted creamy foundation, bronzer, blush, and highlighter on my face, then self-tanner on my limbs and chest. The quieter Leslie straightened, volumized, and sprayed my hair into elegant submission.

“You look stunning,” Brenda said, as she placed brushes, compacts, and tubes back in her travel case.

She gazed over my shoulder into the mirror. My dress was a spectacular work of art, some kind of handkerchief-inspired concoction with muted, metallic colors and wispy trails that draped around my bare legs. It fit my curves perfectly. My bedroom eyes were ringed with smoky shadow and my lips were metallic like my gown. After packing up their paraphernalia, Leslie and Brenda air-kissed me and then disappeared through the front door. Dallas left soon after.

My heartbeat sped up as Mark's arrival approached. I was nervous. When he finally walked through the front door, I went into the foyer to greet him. He was wearing a button-down shirt beneath a crisp, tailored blazer, his pecs outlined beneath the material. He looked tired, a shadow of stubble across his cheeks and a hint of puffiness beneath his eyes. But even looking tired suited him.

He dropped his suitcase onto the floor, his eyes brightening as they met mine. He surveyed me, giving an almost imperceptible nod of approval. He held out his hand to me.

"You okay?"

I walked over to him, letting him wrap an arm around my waist. "Yes."

"Good. The limo is on the way. You can prove to me just how sorry you are." He winked, lifted his bag from the floor, and headed up the stairs.

I resisted the urge to text Dallas to ask what "prove how sorry you are" meant. She wasn't my sex therapist. I would have to navigate this tricky situation all by myself.

When Mark came downstairs fifteen minutes later, he was transformed. His skin and eyes were brighter, his hair was moussed, and he wore a striking black tux that was obviously custom-made. Still, beautiful as he was, he wasn't Teddy. My heart ached for that fact.

Mark strode to the front door and opened it, looking back at me.

"Shall we?" he asked.

I grabbed my Stella clutch from the table in the foyer and nodded, my breath hitching in my chest. Why did it suddenly feel like I was embarking on the limo ride of doom? I approached the vehicle apprehensively, with Mark trailing closely behind. We slid in and the driver headed out of the driveway.

Almost instantly, Mark pressed his body against mine, one of his hands sliding up my thigh while the other clamped around my breast. I was immediately on defense, attempting to pull my body out of his grasp while forcing his insistent hands away.

"You're going to mess up my dress."

Mark pressed his mouth into the side of my neck and began sucking on my skin. It was repellent. "Who cares?" he said.

"Seriously. Can't we do this…*later*?"

He ignored me, slipping a cold hand down the top of my skin-tight bodice. As he fondled my breast unpleasantly, the couture fabric made a ripping sound.

"You're ruining it. *Stop*."

"Oh, come on. It's got a ripped look." Mark ran his tongue along my neck and behind my ear. I shuddered.

"Mark, please. Stop."

He sat back, surveying me through narrowed eyes. "What's the problem? Do you want to tell me something?"

I panted, struggling to catch my breath. "Huh? What do you mean?"

"Are you screwing that white trash rapper?"

"What? *No*."

"Good." Mark shoved his hand hard up my dress once again, his thumb skimming the outside of my panties.

"*Quit*." I shoved his hand away, though he continued to relentlessly push it up my dress.

"You used to be so fun. What happened?"

I was aware that Mark smelled amazing, looked amazing, sounded amazing. *Damn, those Scottish accents.* Yet, no matter how I approached it in my mind, sleeping with Mark would be cheating on Teddy. Regardless of whether Teddy knew who I was in this world or not, I just couldn't do that to him—it would break both of our hearts.

Plus, sophisticated as Mark appeared to be, I had the overwhelming feeling of being groped by a horny teenager—albeit one who was ten years my senior. I glanced up and made eye contact with the driver. Mark couldn't even be bothered to shut the damn privacy screen. I pulled my neck away from his hot breath and pushed against his invading hand, which continued to inch dangerously far up.

I relented for a few seconds, allowing him to knead my thigh too hard while sucking on my neck. It was terribly disgusting. But my irritation built like a boiling kettle. Finally, I couldn't take it anymore.

"I said *stop*."

I shoved Mark with all of the strength in both of my arms, slamming him against the inside of the car door. It just so happened that at that very moment, the door swung open. Mark plummeted backward onto the unforgiving pavement below. I fell onto the ground beside him.

"Oh shit oh shit oh shit!" hissed Denver, who had opened the door. She was still Francesca's assistant in this world.

Denver swiftly yanked me up and dusted off my ten-thousand-dollar gown as an untold number of cameras flashed upon me. Mark stood up, flicked the dirt off his pants, and adjusted his bow-tie indignantly.

He didn't speak to me for the rest of the evening, smiling only when we were posing for photos and sneering at me the rest of the time. The vitriol of his anger seeped into me minute by minute. I realized just how isolated I was in this world.

Ten million adoring fans and yet I was completely alone.

Chapter Seventeen

Skye

I woke up the following morning with a clear plan in mind—it was more like a need than a plan, really. A need to see someone who cared about me. Someone who truly knew me—and loved me.

Shortly after downing a pre-made fried egg and avocado biscuit the chef had left in the fridge, I was driving to Maxie's studio.

It was beginning to feel as if this present reality would break me. Seeing Teddy in a completely new life had filled me with a sense of anxious desperation. It made all of the other little irritations, from Mark relentlessly groping me in the car to Billie using me for press, both meaningless and unbearable.

The address of Maxie's shop was the same, as was the shrill dinging sound of the door as I pulled it open and stepped inside. The familiarity of it all made me feel as if I was momentarily back in my old life.

"Welcome. How can I help you?"

An unfamiliar woman in her early twenties appeared at the front of the store. She had spiky pink hair and about fifteen metal studs in one of her ears. I opened my mouth to speak, then paused. I watched as her expression morphed from neutral to shocked to giddy.

"Oh my gosh, you're—Skye Peters." She caved into herself as she cupped her hands over her mouth. "Oh, wow, sorry. Um, I just…wasn't expecting to see a superstar today. I'm Lucy, by the way." She pressed her shoulders back and fanned her flushed face with one of her hands, attempting to regain her composure.

"No, that's fine," I said, breaking into a smile. I couldn't help myself. Having this effect on people hadn't gotten stale, at least not yet.

I glanced around the space, studying Maxie's work. A massive piece at the front showcased a stunning mix of gold and silver metals, while a wall next to it showcased some smaller paintings—the exposed back of a woman cooking in front of a sunny window; a pair of interlaced fingers on an electric pink background, the skin of one hand rich and amber-colored, the other pasty and stark white.

"I'm a really big fan of Maxie—"

"You are?" The woman's voice cracked as she shuddered.

"Yes. Does she happen to be available? I would love to meet her."

"Yes. Yes, she is. I'll get her." The woman did a sort of dance in place, then ran through the door that led into Maxie's painting area.

While I waited, I strolled through the space, noting which art I recognized and which I didn't. I contemplated how my influence as her friend might have affected which pieces she created.

"Skye? So nice to meet you."

Maxie glided through the door toward me. My heart soared at the sight of her. Beautiful as always, her glowy complexion was ethereal as was her flowing colorblock caftan.

Unsurprisingly she showed zero signs of being starstruck. She was confident and not impressed by celebrity bullshit.

"So I hear you're a fan?" She squeezed my arm and smiled softly. I recognized the familiar spicy scent of her body lotion.

"Yes, I am. I love them all."

I stared into my friend's dark eyes, hoping she would recognize me somehow and rescue me from this loneliness.

"That's so flattering," she said, looking away.

"In fact, I'd like to buy them all." I made a sweeping sound with my arm.

Maxie chuckled. "Oh, that's not necessary. If you wouldn't mind, I'd love for you to share a post on social media. If it appealed to even a fraction of your audience, it could make a huge difference for my art."

I tried not to notice the twinge in my chest. The feeling that Maxie was using me just like so many others.

"Of course…"

"Lucy." Maxie called out to the starstruck clerk who walked over to us.

I handed the woman my phone, then lined up shoulder to shoulder with Maxie. I prayed my smile didn't look forced. Lucy handed my phone back.

"I was also wanting to ask if you'd want to join me for lunch today. I'd love to learn more about your artistic process," I said.

At that moment, a tall woman with a cropped haircut came from the back dragging a rolling suitcase.

"Oh, I'd love to. But my girlfriend and I are

actually heading out for a trip today." She broke out into a smile. "Hawaii. Celebrating some business milestones. And this is even more reason to celebrate."

I stepped back to allow her girlfriend past.

"We actually have to go right now. It was so nice to meet you though. Stop back by in a few weeks when I return."

Maxie gave a little wave and disappeared through the door. The store felt painfully lonely in her wake.

"Will you be taking everything with you or should I have it shipped to your address?" Lucy asked.

I had attempted to buy Maxie's friendship and failed miserably.

"Ship it," I said, heading towards the exit.

Chapter Eighteen

Skye

After my failed attempt at connecting with Maxie, I made the decision to see Teddy's next show. Just a few days later I found myself inside the GBC Towers, the glass skyscraper where *Tunes by Teddy*, as well as a popular late show and a sketch comedy program, were filmed. I was dressed casually in slim, straight-leg jeans and a simple tee, a baseball cap low over my blonde ponytail. I prayed not to be recognized. Then I slid inside one of the many cars at my disposal and snuck away.

There was a line outside of Studio 4B, where *Tunes by Teddy* was shot. People stood quietly chatting between two red velvet ropes. For every adult, there was at least one child, many dancing excitedly on tip-toes or jumping up and down, giddy with anticipation. After about thirty minutes, we were ushered into the cool, dark studio. I was immediately hit by a cold gush of air.

The audience members remained in a tight line as we were directed to our seats. I took my place in the back row. I didn't mind being so far away from the stage. I could still see Teddy, but it would mean there was less of a chance I would be recognized.

After more waiting around as people filed in, I

heard a stirring around me. I looked up to find Caroline below us on the stage. She wore a black headset and a monitor clipped to her waistband.

"Hi, everyone. Welcome to *Tunes by Teddy*. We're thrilled to have you with us today." She raised her hands over her head and clapped, a signal for all of us to clap as well. "Very soon, Teddy himself will be coming out to sing for you—" A few whoops sounded from around me. "—But, first, I want to make sure you're all properly pumped up for the awesomeness you're about to experience. See this sign above my head?" Caroline pointed to a lit-up "Applause" sign high up on the wall to her left. Everyone clapped in reply. "Each time you see that sign light up, I need you to clap your hands together as loudly as you've ever clapped them before. Got it?"

"Got it!" the audience shouted back.

"Okay," Caroline said as the light flicked off. "Let's practice. Is everyone ready to have some fun?"

At that moment, the sign lit up and a mediocre smattering of applause followed.

Caroline scrunched up her face. "That was *okay*," she said, drawing out the last word. "But I think we can do better. Let's try it again. *Is everyone ready to have some fun?*"

This time, the applause was much louder and there were a few whoops of excitement thrown in as well—no thanks to my tepid claps. I wasn't about to go along with anything Caroline suggested. If she so much as recommended I breathe, I'd try to stop inhaling and consider whether there was a better way to survive.

"That's more like it," she shouted, a serene smile overtaking her face. "Okay, it's almost time now. Sit tight and Teddy will be out soon."

I watched Caroline exit the stage. Thanks to her, every time I saw a woman with a pixie cut, I wanted to throw up all over them. The haircut itself seemed mocking and irritating—though that was probably just Caroline.

"Have you seen this show before?"

A sweet, small voice broke through my internal seething. I turned to find a girl of about eight in the seat next to me.

"Oh…yes, um, once or twice."

"*In person?*" The girl's twinkling eyes widened.

"Um, yes, I, uh, work nearby here," I lied.

"I just *love Tunes by Teddy*. I know all of his songs, especially 'Puppy in my Pocket'."

I smiled, recognizing the song title. "*Ah*, that's one of my favorites, too."

"Do you have any kids?" she asked.

"Oh, um, no." Then, pondering the question a bit more, I realized that actually wasn't true. "Oh, yes, I do…two."

The girl cocked an eyebrow at me, clearly confused as to why I had forgotten my two children.

A palpable ripple of excitement abruptly moved through the crowd. I turned to find Teddy strolling onto the stage.

"*Ohhh,*" the girl next to me squealed, as the lights around us dimmed.

The children in the audience let out a smattering of screams and hollers, claps and whoops. I twisted in my seat to get a better view of him. My Teddy.

"Hi, everyone," he said. "Thank you so much for coming to the show today. It's going to be a great one.

If you have any special requests, we'll save time for them at the very end of the show. But if you're all ready for some *Tunes by Teddy*—" Shrieks of excitement ensued. "—let's do it."

"Aren't you forgetting someone?" a high-pitched, squeaky voice interrupted.

At the appearance of Teddy's puppet sidekick, the children again erupted in another wave of excitement.

Teddy's eyes got wide and he raised his eyebrows in mock embarrassment. "Oh, sorry, Griffin. I didn't mean to start the show without you."

"That's fine," Griffin said, clearing his voice. "Let's do this."

I scanned the edges of the stage and saw Caroline standing there, in the same place she stood in the other reality. The reality where Teddy and I were together. She watched him with rapt attention, studying his every move, until a production assistant ran up beside her and they began looking over something on her clipboard.

Teddy breezed through a series of songs, tapping his foot as he sang. I recognized all but one of them. Seeing Teddy through the eyes of my new self was strange. Instead of comfort and familiarity—feelings Teddy usually stirred in me—I felt longing. I saw his sparkling dark eyes, strong nose, and fluid movement with unvarnished clarity. After performing four songs, Teddy reached out long, tanned fingers to clutch the glass of water sitting on a bench to his right. He put the glass to his lips.

"So," Griffin said in a high-pitched, uneven tone. "Don't you have any songs about squirrels?"

Teddy froze and gave the audience a pointed look. Slowly, he returned the glass to the bench. "So, you're a *squirrel*, Griffin?"

It was an on-going joke that Teddy wasn't sure what kind of animal Griffin was.

"What?" Griffin said. "I most certainly am not. Why would you think a silly thing like that?"

Children's laughter erupted from the audience.

"Oh," Teddy replied. "No, of course not. And no—I don't have any songs about squirrels. But I do have one about…*hedgehogs*!" Teddy shouted the last word as if he was again guessing Griffin's species.

"Okay, sure," Griffin said, sounding bored.

Teddy slumped his shoulders in disappointment for a moment, then popped them back up and returned to his normal upbeat state. In my previous existence, I had grown increasingly annoyed at Teddy's affable cheer. From my new vantage point, it was endearing, adorable—and impressive. Who had the emotional reserve to stay so consistent?

As Teddy strummed his fingers across the strings of his guitar, I sensed someone's gaze on me. I tensed up, then slowly turned to my left. The little girl was staring at me. Her eyes were huge, and her mouth gaped open. The skin on my face danced with prickles and my heart jackhammered in my ribs. After the lights had dimmed and I had gotten lost in Teddy's performance, I had taken off my hat, revealing my blonde hair. Letting my guard down was a bad idea. Did the little girl recognize me? I swallowed a lump in my throat as she continued to stare.

"Um…are you okay?" I asked her.

"*It's you.*"

"Hmmm? No, it's not, uh—"

"It's you!" This time she shouted the words and

followed up her exclamation with an ear-piercing squeal.

My cheeks burned as I sunk into the wobbly velvet chair. Had anyone heard her? My question was immediately answered when the family in front of us turned to stare with a mixture of irritation and curiosity. Suddenly, Teddy's song stopped. *Shit.*

Confusion and concern spread across the audience and crew. Everyone turned to peer into the back row. A few people even stood up to get a better view.

"It's her," someone yelled. "It's Skye Peters!"

Shrieks of excitement erupted like tiny bombs spread across the audience. Two small girls a row ahead of me turned beet red as they stood in their seats. They brought their hands to their mouths as they exchanged looks. The expression of a mother in front of me morphed from irritation to reverence.

"What's that I hear?" Teddy's voice rang clearly through the studio. "Is that *Countdown to Famous* winner Skye Peters in the back row?"

I sunk into my seat, my head lower than the little girl who had started all this chaos. But there was no use in trying to disappear. Everyone now seemed to be waiting for me to respond. After a few painfully prolonged seconds, I finally rose from my seat. I locked eyes with Teddy, who was standing at the front of the stage, a hand resting on his guitar. Beyond him, Caroline clutched her clipboard so tightly, her fingers had turned white. It was as if she was holding herself back from jumping onto the stage.

I lifted my hand and gave Teddy a quick wave.

"Um, yes, hello…that's me." My cheeks were red-hot as I smiled and shrugged.

Teddy gazed at me, the chaos around us descending into the background. Only he and I remained now. Had his eyes always been so deep, so intense? In them, I was certain I saw recognition—not just of me as a celebrity, but of something deeper existing between us.

"Well, Skye," he finally said. "Would you care to join me onstage for a song?"

"Yes, Skye!" "Please sing for us, Skye!" "Yesyesyes!" Voices rose up from the audience.

"Sure, why not?" Heart hammering in my chest, I scooted toward the aisle, the people around allowing me to pass as if I was the Queen of England.

I could feel the hot stare of every audience member as I made my way down the stairs. I glanced at my outfit, evaluating whether it was suitable for the stage. Though jeans and a T-shirt were not my typical stage attire, they hugged my curves. They would have to do.

Teddy stepped forward to the edge of the stage, leaning forward to reach a hand down to me. I peered into his eyes as I took it. His skin was ice cold, causing a jolt through me. I smiled. His hands were always cold.

"Sorry," he said, pulling me onto the stage.

We gazed at each other. It was as if we were communicating without speaking. Did he know who I really was? Could he feel it?

Teddy removed the water glass from the wooden bench, then pulled the bench forward and motioned for me to sit down.

"Thank you," I said as Teddy stood beside me.

"Is there a special song you'd like to sing?" Teddy's wide smile took up half of his tanned face. He exuded genuine warmth.

I stared into the darkened studio audience. It was slightly less intimidating now that I had performed in front of thousands of people. Still, my heart pounded in my ribcage.

"How about 'Together Again'?"

Teddy's smile vanished, and he squinted at me in disbelief. Then his smile came back. "You know my songs?"

"A couple…I have…stepchildren…"

"Oh, of course. All right. Let's do it."

Teddy began tapping out a beat on his leg. "*Shoe-do, dobie-do, dobie-shoe.*"

"Though the nights may be dark, though the days may be long," I sang, again surprised at the even, powerful tone of my voice. *"Though the trees may be thick and the words may be wrong. Remember this one thing if you're ever low. I love you, love you, love you more than you know."*

"I love you, love you, love you more than you know," Teddy sang. *"Some days are sad, but good days will come soon. Just wish on the stars and follow the moon..."*

As Teddy sang, I glanced over and found him staring back. His eyes twinkled with emotion. We remained like that—locked in each other's eyes—for several seconds. Seconds that felt like hours. Singing with him was incredible. How had we never done this before? How was that possible? We *were* both singers, after all. Except—in my previous life—I didn't think of myself as a singer and no one else did either.

After we finished the song, the audience sprung to their feet and clapped furiously. They cried out for us to continue.

"More!"

I felt Teddy's warm, strong hand press against my lower back before I realized he had moved close. Something electric shot through me. "Thanks so much for singing with me." He spoke the words low into my ear, his spearmint-scented breath cool against my neck. "I better get back on task or my producer will murder me." We both glanced at Caroline, whose narrowed eyes watched us from the side of the stage.

"Of course." I began to step away, but he spoke again.

"But could you do me a favor first?"

My heart thumped loudly at this suggestion. Was he going to ask for my phone number? To see me again? Maybe everything would start to make sense.

"Yes," I breathed.

"My wife is a huge fan of yours. Could we all get a selfie together?"

My skin went cold. "Of course."

Teddy stepped away, motioning to someone in the audience. A woman, brunette and shorter than me, stepped forward. She cupped her hands over her mouth as she half-ran toward the stage.

Before I could process anything, the woman's hand was on my shoulder and the scent of her perfume, bittersweet, attacked my nostrils. A string of words I couldn't comprehend escaped her lips. "Such a fan…thrilled…thank you."

I didn't try to understand or respond. Instead, I simply posed between the two of them, my almost-fiancé and his wife, and bared my teeth into what I hoped resembled a smile as a production assistant shouted "*Cheese*" and held up a phone.

Seconds later, I was saying good-bye to Teddy and his wife as they escorted me off the stage. I walked in the direction of my seat, but as I reached the last aisle I continued forward, into the depths of the studio, and all the way through the exit door.

Chapter Nineteen

Skye

By the time I got back to the car, I was shaking uncontrollably. I dove into the driver's seat, slamming the door shut behind me. As I hunched over the steering wheel, I ceased holding back my tears and let them fall freely over my cheeks.

I fumbled with my phone, sliding my fingers around the screen without seeing. When my eyes finally focused, I saw the red number on my text message icon was unusually large, even for this new life. I clicked the icon and read through the messages from Dallas. There were seven.

—SOS. Come home now.—

—Where are you?—

—Francesca's on the way. Emergency meeting.—

—Are you coming?—

—She's here!—

—Where are you?? Are you okay??—

—Don't read the news.—

I immediately closed the text messages app and clicked into the web browser, which was already opened to my go-to celebrity gossip site. As I enlarged the app, the main homepage image came into view. A ball of phlegm rose up in my throat. I knew instantly who it was.

There was a slideshow of slightly blurry images, likely taken from some distance. They were all of Mark and Monika Earl, his most recent ingénue—a photo of Mark stroking the bare skin under her crop top, one of Monika leaning against him as they strolled in a dark parking lot, another of the two of them kissing in front of a neon-lit nightclub as he tilted her chin upward.

That asshole. While it was true I didn't love Mark, it was also true he had made a complete joke of me. He had lied to my face—he even had the gall to make me feel guilty over Billie. My body burned as I ground my teeth together.

I pictured Comet and Lucienne and a twinge in my chest made me feel weak. They would see this too. They would have to go through another divorce because of their dad's complete inability to remain loyal and committed to one woman. Because their dad was a selfish, thoughtless prick. They didn't deserve this.

When I walked into the house nearly an hour later, my head was spinning with thoughts of Teddy and his wife mixed in with Mark and Monika. Dallas, Francesca, and Denver each paced my kitchen, catlike. The breakfast table was crammed with three laptops, a tablet, and a series of disposable coffee cups.

"*Honey.*" Francesca hurried toward me with open arms. Her voice was saccharin. "I'm *so* sorry. But we're going to fix this." Her glossy black hair had a slight wave, and she wore a loose navy shirt and palazzo pants. She used her cold, bony fingers to press my head upon her equally bony shoulder.

Behind her, Denver and Dallas paused beside the table. Dallas's eyes were wide under raised brows and her mouth seemed to be forming a word she couldn't get out. Francesca released me, marched back to the table, and placed a finger on the keyboard of one of the laptops.

"The head of the label, Brendan Mullins, just called. He wants to make sure they're doing all they can to get ahead of this thing—*so* smart of him. Of course we were just doing clean-up over the Billie Bird mess. Now *this*." She paused, eliciting a weary sigh as she swept a strand of hair from her face. "I set up a meeting with him for the first thing tomorrow morning. I told Brendan I would come too, but he insisted it be just you—says he wants to keep it more informal."

I shrugged, placing my purse on the counter.

"You've been gone for a while," Denver said. "What were you up to?"

All three of them stared expectantly.

"Just running errands." I swallowed. I had no desire to explain why I had been to see a barely famous children's singer, though it was likely to show up online before too long.

Denver and Francesca exchanged a look.

"Can you get me a glass of Prosecco?" I asked Dallas. She nodded and hurried around Denver toward the refrigerator as my phone began buzzing. My breath caught when I saw the name on the screen. My jaw set, I jerked the phone to my ear.

"Skye?" Mark said. "What's going on? I tried to get into the house and Francesca had one of the drivers force me out. She said they were changing the locks to the house."

"*What's going on*, Mark? *Really*? What's going on is that you've been cheating on me for months and you finally got caught."

My raw emotions were caused by Teddy—I couldn't care less about Mark beyond my own bruised ego. Still, this situation served as an appropriate outlet for my despair.

There was silence on the other end for a few moments, followed by a sigh. "Listen, Freckles—"

"*Don't call me Freckles.*"

"Okay. Listen. I know I shouldn't have gotten caught—"

"—*gotten caught?* What about not cheating in the first place?"

"C'mon, think about our careers, Skye. Do the smart thing here. Don't let your emotions rule the show. You're better than that. I know you are."

"Screw you." I experienced a jolt of satisfaction as I realized I would no longer have to think up ways to avoid sex with him.

"It's my house too."

"Doesn't Monika have a place you can stay?" Silence. "Go to hell, Mark." I hung up and tossed the phone in my bag.

"Good job, girl." Denver pumped her fist in the air. As usual, she looked like she'd stepped off the pages of a fashion magazine with her glossy blonde bob and flawless designer dress.

"Are you okay?" Dallas fluttered around me, pushing a chilled glass of white wine into my hand.

"I'm fine." I glanced at the three women, all wearing doubtful expressions. "I promise."

"This is going to be great for you, darling," Francesca said, turning to her laptop screen. "I'm going to book you multiple covers. We're going to position you as the phoenix rising from the ashes. As the girl who can never be knocked down. You'll be an inspiration. In fact, I think this is the best thing that could have happened to you."

When Francesca finally looked up, Denver, Dallas and I were staring at her, our mouths agape.

"Too soon?" She elicited a pseudo-embarrassed chuckle. "Sorry."

"I'm going to bed." I lifted my bag from the table and headed in the direction of my bedroom, wine in hand.

"Don't forget your meeting with Brendan tomorrow at eight a.m. sharp," Francesca called after me.

I dragged my feet into the master bedroom and shut the door. I yanked the curtains closed, blocking what remained of the daylight, then peeled off the jeans and tee and crawled beneath the sheet and comforter in my bra and underwear.

In the silence of the room, something weighed heavy on my chest. Today had been an undeniable reminder: Teddy was not mine. At least not in this world. I couldn't shake the feeling this was some kind of punishment. After all, I had fallen into this alternate reality while attempting to avoid his proposal. What would I give to have that chance again…right this very instant?

Seeing things from this perspective made it obvious how much I wanted to be with Teddy. How much I wanted to be the one having a baby with Teddy. Meeting pop stars with Teddy. Screw *being* the pop star. That didn't feel nearly as good as it looked.

Loneliness spread over me like black ink bleeding onto a white sheet. I tugged the covers up to my chin and burrowed my unwashed skin into the pillow. I had to face the fact that I may never go back to my old life. I had no idea how I got *here*, and I had no idea how to get back *there*. Exhausted and weak, I soon fell into a sleep that was both agitated and deep.

Chapter Twenty

Caroline - One week earlier

“Was that as good for you as it was for me?”

At his question, I glanced over at the sweaty, red-faced man reclining next to me in bed and wrinkled my nose. I had found him online, and I was relatively satisfied. He was at least six-two, with wide shoulders and symmetrical features. I had found that sometimes when you feel shitty, you just need to hook up with a perfect stranger. It can help. It *has* helped. Yet this was about far more than just lifting my mood.

I pushed up and flung my legs over the edge of my bed, still stark naked. I was no longer able to resist what had been on my mind for the past few hours. I jerked open my nightstand drawer and pulled out my Glock 32 pistol. It was loaded.

“Shit.” The man’s eyes widened as he caught sight of the pistol. He hurled himself out of bed, doing a little hop to avoid tripping over the covers he had dragged onto the hardwood. “Did I do something to upset you?”

He laughed at his own joke. I rolled my eyes.

Standing in only tighty-whities before me, I was able to more thoroughly survey the stranger’s body. It was fleshy and covered with blondish hair. His splotchy skin was slowly losing its redness. I could only imagine what Ted would look like standing undressed before me. Something flamed low in my stomach.

“You were fine.” I stared at him, unsmiling.

“Okay…” He looked at me from the corner of his eye, then leaned forward and quickly pulled on the jeans he had left piled in a chair. “Then why the hell are you holding a gun?”

I turned back to look at my Glock, all black and silver metal. Small and delicate. Powerful and merciless. I loved this gun.

“To protect myself, obviously. But I do have a little proposition for you.”

The man slid into his Hawaiian shirt and began buttoning it up, never taking his eyes off me or the gun.

“Should’ve known I would meet another crazy psycho online…”

“I did some research on you before we met tonight. I know you have several misdemeanors. Class C was the latest. So don’t act like you’re a law-abiding citizen.”

“What does that have to do with anything?”

“My proposition. It comes with ten thousand dollars for you.”

The man turned to leave. His hand hovered over the bedroom door handle, then abruptly dropped. He turned to face me, his shirt partially unbuttoned and revealing unsightly blond chest hair.

“To do what?” he said. “And with that tiny-ass gun?”

I stood, pulled on my bra and panties, and walked around the bed. I held the gun reverently. “Yes. Unless you have another one you want to use.”

The man pressed himself against the closed bedroom door, pushing his chin into his neck as he eyed the gun nervously. I spread my legs wide apart directly across from him. “I want you to shoot someone.”

The man’s face flushed red. He laughed humorously. “Kill someone?”

“Ideally. Five before and five when it’s done.”

“Who? Nobody famous?”

“No. She’s nobody famous. She’s a total nobody. The world would be better off—”

“Yeah, yeah, yeah,” he said. “I’ll do it.”

I pulled my light cotton robe off the edge of the chair and slid into it.

“Wait right here.”

I moved past him into the hallway and headed toward the safe to get the first installment of cash. There was a distinct feeling of lightness in my chest.

I was doing it. I was taking my future into my own hands. A future that would now include my Ted.

Chapter Twenty-One

Skye

"This is not good." Brendan Mullins stood behind his massive mahogany desk the following morning, hands placed low on sharp hips.

The record executive's luxe seventeenth-floor office showcased an expansive view of downtown Los Angeles. The space gushed with expensive everything—cushy brown leather chairs, an intricate Turkish rug in pastel hues, and original artwork featuring angry red swoops and swirls.

Brendan himself had thick brown hair and well-maintained eyebrows. His silver-gray suit was perfectly tailored, and his shiny leather dress shoes looked as if they'd never been worn. Brendan struck me as someone who would be escorted from the office straight to the gym, where his expensive personal trainer awaited, then to cocktails at some exclusive dinner club.

Sitting cross-legged in one of the leather chairs, I surveyed two gold frames on his desk. One featured a young woman with thick blonde hair and red lips. She fit the stereotype of his wife: thin, well-dressed, attractive. The other frame displayed a boy and a girl splashing giddily in a gushing sprinkler, drops of water catching the afternoon sunlight. His children, most likely. I imagined they were enrolled in the top private schools en route to the Ivy League.

"But we can work something out, can't we?" Brendan said.

As I glanced up at him, he tilted his chin downward and lifted his eyebrows. A smirk danced on his lips. I turned away and gazed out the window, repelled by what he was suggesting. Or was I misreading things? I studied the sunlight glinting over the tiny metal structures below us.

"What can I do? Mark's the one who needs to fix something."

Brendan inhaled sharply and sauntered around the front of the desk. He perched on its edge so he was positioned directly across and slightly above me. He stacked one hand over the other on his right hip and stared at me intensely.

"But that's not how the game works. You've been in this business long enough to know that, my dear. Come on." He reached down and clamped a cold, dry hand around my thigh, which was bare beneath a plaid shirtdress.

I froze. How close *were* we? Was this normal in the record industry? Was I sleeping with this man?

"Damn, you're uptight," he said.

Brendan stood again and sauntered around the back of my leather chair. I stiffened as he leaned toward me, kneading his sharp fingertips into my shoulders. His hot breath dampened the top of my hair. "Relax, doll."

"Ow. That hurts." I shrugged away from his hands, a chill spreading through me.

Making a sound of exhaustion, Brendan walked across the office to the wall of windows and began pacing back and forth.

"I understand you're upset about Mark," he said. "But—c'mon. You never really loved him anyway. At least that's what you told me that weekend in New York, right?" He winked and licked his lips, then walked back across the office to stand in front of me.

New York? In this life, was I cheating on Mark with…*him*?

Brendan shrugged off his suit jacket, folded it, and placed it neatly over the front of his desk. Then he unbuttoned the cuffs of his sleeves and slowly rolled them up. I registered each of his actions a few seconds too late, as if there was a delay in my perception.

I was practically paralyzed as he unbuckled his brown leather belt and bent over to slide off his suit pants in one smooth motion. An iciness bled through me. My brain told me to move, but my limbs felt as if they were filled with concrete. Brendan grabbed me and pulled me toward him. I resisted with all my strength, my back pressing hard against his hand.

"What the hell are you doing?" I asked. I struggled to stand, but the depth of the chair combined with Brendan's strength made it impossible. "*Get away from me.*"

I reached out and shoved him hard in the kidney.

"What the *fuck*." Brendan grabbed my arms and tried to force them down, but I fought him with every fiber of my being. I was finally able to rip my arms out of his grasp and claw my way over the back of the chair.

"What do you think you're doing?" he spat. He examined his stomach for injuries as I paused at the door. "You think you'll get away with this? You think I don't *own* you? You think you'll have a career left when I'm done with you?" He laughed humorlessly, pulled up his pants in one swift jerk, and adjusted his collar. "You're gonna be sorry. Get the hell out of my sight."

My heartbeat jackhammering in my ribcage, I fled the room. The attractive blonde assistant outside eyed me, a deep line creasing the space between her microbladed eyebrows.

The half-full lobby seemed to circle around me as if it was on a turntable. I exhaled in rapid, ragged breaths. Clutching my chest, I feared I might collapse. Thankfully, I spotted a women's restroom and escaped into it, leaning my entire weight against the cold countertop.

What in the hell had just happened? Had I been assaulted? Or was I a willing participant, albeit unknowingly? Was *that* the real price of success—having sex with, and being wanted by, the men in charge? Even having incredible talent or pure luck couldn't protect you. In fact, maybe it put a big target on your head. I was confused and weary.

I squeaked on the cold water, leaned over the sink, and splashed my face. What awful thing awaited me next in this facade of a life? I yanked out a paper towel and patted the droplets wetting my face, squeezing my eyes shut and swallowing deep gulps of air.

Suddenly a stall door squeaked open and I sensed someone standing nearby. I opened my eyes to find a twenty-something woman staring at me, eyes wide.

"Oh my God. Skye—*Skye Peters*? I'm a huge fan. Can I get a selfie with you, *please*?"

I wadded up the damp paper towel, pushed down the raw sense of shock reverberating through me, and turned the corners of my lips into a painful smile.

"Of course."

I waited, watching the woman fumble with her phone. Then I leaned in and kept my expression frozen as she clicked several shots.

"See? These look great," she said, holding up the photos to me.

Surprisingly, I looked fairly normal. No one would be able to discern the truth—that I was rapidly falling apart.

"Just enjoy your life. Don't wish for mine. Everything isn't as it appears."

I exited the bathroom, leaving the fan gaping in my wake.

Chapter Twenty-Two

Skye

"Um, maybe don't read the news today."

At Dallas's comment, I glanced up from my bowl of milk and Cheerios. We were sitting together in the breakfast nook. I let the spoon drop into my bowl with a reverberating clank, then pulled my phone off the edge of the table. I unlocked it and went directly to the web.

"Okay," Dallas said. "Well, if you insist—there are some pretty awful things being circulated out there." She cleared her throat, as if considering whether to share exactly what they were.

It had been almost two weeks since Brendan had unsuccessfully tried to feel me up. The negative stories had come out like a small trickle at first, progressing into an overflowing gush.

I googled my name. The top result was of a video showing a woman I didn't recognize being interviewed. The headline read: "Billie Bird's Ex Claims Skye Peters Gave Him STD."

I spit a mouthful of milk and partially chewed cereal back into my bowl.

"*Really? I* gave *him* something? Billie's about the most promiscuous—" I gritted my teeth as Dallas held up a hand to silence me.

"I honestly don't think it's good for your mental

health to read any of this. Please. Don't do it."

I clicked off my phone screen, closed my eyes, and forced myself to take a slow, steady inhale.

"Anyway," Dallas continued. "You have enough to deal with today."

It was mere seconds later when the doorbell's melody was followed by pounding on the front door.

"There she is. Should I?" Dallas said.

I wiped the corners of my mouth with a napkin. "No. I'll do it."

Feeling as if my legs were anchored with weights, I dragged myself to the front door, inhaled sharply, and opened it. JoJo stood on my porch, her eyes narrowed and a balled-up fist resting on her hip. Lucienne and Comet lingered in the yard beyond her. Behind them, two bulky men hopped out of the cab of a moving truck.

"Since you and Mark are no longer a *thing*," JoJo said, clearly not feeling the need for the usual pleasantries. "My children will no longer be living here."

I shrugged as the two movers sauntered up the U-shaped drive toward us. "That's fine." I glanced past her at the kids. Lucienne's arms were wrapped protectively around her stomach as she gazed at the ground. Comet's eyes were enormous and questioning. "Hi, guys," I said, giving them a wave and a weak smile. They each responded with a barely perceptible nod.

"May we?" JoJo said, as the movers came to stand behind her.

I stepped onto the porch and let the three of them pass. As JoJo led the men upstairs, she began listing off the preferred order of tasks for the day. When they were out of sight, I walked into the front yard.

"I'm sorry, guys. I wish this wasn't happening."

Comet looked at me through the sides of his eyes, his face reddening as his eyes filled with tears. I stepped up to him and wrapped him in my arms.

"Everything's going to be okay," I said.

After a few seconds, he pulled away, roughly brushing away the tears on his cheeks. "Thanks."

"It's not your fault." Lucienne examined her nails.

"I know. But I'm sorry anyway. And I want you both to know I am still here for you. Anytime you need anything. You can talk to me. Okay?" I looked from Lucienne to Comet and back again. They both nodded, a hint of relief evident on their faces. "You can't control your dad's stupid mistakes. But, unfortunately, you're affected by them."

Lucienne glanced up, one corner of her mouth inching upward. "Thanks."

A sharp scraping sound caused us all to look up. JoJo had opened Lucienne's second-floor window and was staring through the screen at us.

"Come on, guys. These boxes aren't going to pack themselves." Her eyes shifted to me. "And the faster we get this done, the faster we can get out of here and go get something to eat."

Lucienne sighed heavily and dragged her feet through the grass toward the front door. Comet trailed behind, turning back to me once his sister had disappeared through the doorway.

"Skye?"

"Yes?" I looked up, smiling encouragingly.

"You're different."

My eyebrows scrunched together as I tried to discern his meaning.

"You're not like you used to be," he said. "It's almost like…you're a different person."

I forced a laugh. "Ha. What did I used to be like?"

"Mean."

A stitch in my chest made it hard to inhale. "Wow, that sucks. Sorry about that."

Comet shrugged. "Well, see you around." He disappeared into the house.

The sound of the cell phone in my pocket made me jump. It was a number I didn't recognize, but some unnamed instinct made me pick it up.

"Skye, this is Caroline, Ted Sorens's producer."

I swallowed, eyes fixed at the row of trees along the property's edge. "Uh-huh…"

"Ted has received an offer to perform on *Good Morning, USA* next week…if it's a duet with you." I could hear her irritated exhale on the other end. "I assume you know the video of you singing with Ted has gone viral? Anyway, can we count on you to be available? I'll send over the details."

The idea of helping Teddy's career, helping him in any way, caused my heartbeat to thump harder and faster in my chest. "Yes. I'll do it. I'll have my assistant reach out."

"Perfect. Good day."

I started toward the house, but stopped when my phone began wailing again. This time I knew exactly who it was. Francesca. Seeing her name on my phone screen filled me with an inexplicable sense of dread.

"Hello?" My tone was meek and barely audible. Francesca pounced immediately.

"Why the hell haven't you been answering your phone? I've been trying to call you for the last half-hour. Listen—I've gotten multiple calls from news sites asking for comments."

"What—I didn't see your calls…a comment on what?"

"Take your pick. Any number of stories. Is it true that your voice has turned to gravel and Brendan isn't renewing your contract? Which, according to Brendan, he isn't. Oh, and this is a good one. Did you give Mark herpes—is that why he cheated on you?"

"What? Brendan made a pass at me so I reacted as anyone would. I told him to screw off. And give Mark herpes? *Please*. According to these liars, I've been giving the whole city STDs."

Francesca was silent for several seconds. "I don't need to know the details of your personal life. I know Brendan and you had a *thing*. I also know I've been working my *ass* off to spin this in your direction and you just shit all over it."

"We had a thing?" I was shouting now, my fist clenched at my side. "Whatever *thing* Brendan and I had was transactional and predatory and should never have happened."

"Listen." Francesca's voice was low and full of vitriol. "If you don't do your job, I can't do mine. Pepperlake PR can no longer represent you. Our contract is officially terminated. Good luck to you."

Click.

I slid the phone back in my pocket, suddenly aware my hands were shaking. Who cared if one of the hundreds of PR people in LA wouldn't represent me? I was the biggest star on the planet…at least one of the biggest in the United States. Surely, any PR professional would clamor to help me out.

I walked inside and directly to my bedroom, turned out the light, and lay down to take a nap. When the sound of knocking woke me up, I was disoriented and unsure how long I had been sleeping.

"Skye?"

I lifted my head, peering toward the door with bleary eyes. Lucienne was standing in the doorway, Comet behind her.

"We're leaving," she said, taking a tentative step inside the darkened room.

I struggled to get up, rubbing the sleep from my eyes as I closed the distance between us.

"You're all done packing?"

I took in the two children—twelve and eight—who appeared even younger as they looked at me with wide, worried eyes.

"I'll miss you guys."

I wrapped my arms around Lucienne first, then Comet, pulling them both close.

"We'll miss you too." Lucienne took a step back and stared at the ground.

An awkward silence filled the space between as I searched for something comforting to say.

"Mom's waiting in the car," Lucienne finally said. "We better go."

"Of course."

I followed them to the front door and watched as they walked to the car, waving as they drove out of sight.

"You okay?" Dallas squeezed my shoulder as I stared out the front door.

"I'm good." I shut the door and turned toward her. "You should go home. There's nothing else going on today. You deserve a break."

Dallas raised her eyebrows. "Really? Well, okay. I might take you up on that."

Once Dallas was gone, I stood in the kitchen and listened, truly understanding the term "deafening silence" for the first time. I walked into the living room, where I had first fallen into this world. I peered into the office where I had searched and discovered just who I was in this new life. I meandered upstairs to the master bedroom still filled with Mark's belongings and then into Lucienne and Comet's former bedrooms, completely empty except for dust bunnies, candy wrappers, and a few cords.

The late afternoon light filtered through the windows, giving everything a yellowed, antique tint. An inescapable restlessness gnawed at my core. I was unable to sit, to rest, to focus.

Finally I grabbed my bag and headed toward the garage. If only I had been able to endure the stillness, maybe then I wouldn't have made things inexplicably worse.

Chapter Twenty-Three

Skye

I drove through the streets of L.A. for almost an hour, a blur of images and emotions racing through my mind and body. I felt better being out of the house, but exhaustion weighed on me. All I wanted to do was sleep, but I also couldn't bear the thought of returning to the cavernous mansion that now held nobody but me and me alone.

Finally, I pulled into a Louie's Chicken restaurant, craving some french fries and a sickeningly sweet soda. Sitting unnoticed in the corner of a lively restaurant sounded appealing. Blending into the background while also being part of the crowd.

A man and his two daughters were just stepping away from the counter when I pushed in through the entrance, a bell signaling my arrival. I wore my baseball cap and kept my head down as I passed the family, careful not to be noticed. I couldn't handle smiling for the fans right now. I just didn't have the mental energy.

I approached a woman in her early twenties who was standing behind the counter. She wore the fast food chain's familiar blue-and-white apron, her dark hair pulled into a ponytail beneath the matching visor.

She glanced up at me as I stood in front of her, then

looked back down at her phone. I watched her for a few minutes as she chomped on a large chunk of gum.

"*Ahem*."

She looked up, anger flashing in her eyes. "Don't clear your throat at me," she said.

Rage shot through me. "*Excuse me*? I've been standing here waiting for you to take my order while you purposely ignore me. Could you be any more *rude*?"

The woman glared at me. "You need to shut your mouth, *perra*."

Was this chick for real? I ripped off my baseball cap and slammed it onto the counter between us. "Do you know who I am? Ever heard of me?"

The woman's face went slack.

"That's right. Skye Peters. Multi-Sonny winning pop star. So get your head out of your ass and take my freaking order."

"Oh," she mumbled. "What would you like?"

"Fries and a soda." I breathed out in a gush of air as the woman tapped my order in.

Before I could feel a speck of remorse, I sensed something in my peripheral vision. I turned. A short man in a long T-shirt held up a phone several feet away. Two other people did the same. I was being recorded from all angles.

A coldness bled through me. This was not good.

****

The following day, Dallas and I monitored the news as increasingly angry stories came out regarding my restaurant outburst. By the end of the day, the top analysis of it all was that I was a racist because the clerk was Latina and I was white. Of course that was a complete untruth. Still, I couldn't help but feel ashamed of the way I had acted. Of the way I had treated the clerk.

A week later, millions got a laugh at my expense as *Friday Night Comics* did a skit where a spoiled blonde screamed "I'm a Multi-Sonny winning pop star" and promptly transformed into a monster who smashed the restaurant into pieces. Around that same time, I received a text from Caroline canceling my proposed duet with Teddy on *Good Morning, USA.* It had been the one thing I had been looking forward to, seeing Teddy again. The loss of it was crushing.

To top everything off, I was dealing with this nightmare without the help of a PR team. Dallas told me a few people had reached out to offer their services, but I didn't feel capable of making a good decision. Not with the whirlwind in my heart and head.

Finally, a few weeks after the incident, Dallas decided we needed to take action. I had turned down all interview requests for fear of making things worse. But that certainly hadn't improved things.

"You need to put out a statement. In your own words."

It felt like Dallas was my one true friend in the world. I was so thankful for her at that moment.

"Admit you were wrong," she said. "Because *you were wrong.*"

And that's how I found myself staring into a camera, a light ring illuminating my complexion, as I tried to speak from the heart.

"I'm deeply ashamed of my behavior," I said, my voice shaky. "It had absolutely nothing to do with the ethnicity of the woman I verbally attacked, who I have apologized to. Absolutely all forms of racism are despicable. It was more about…I've discovered it's a lot easier to hurt others when you yourself are hurting. To lash out at others and excuse that behavior when really it's completely inexcusable." I inhaled, proceeding. "And furthermore I've placed way too much emphasis on fame, outward validation, and appearances. I'm sorry for my behavior. It was unacceptable and I'm terribly remorseful and embarrassed."

I felt suddenly lightheaded and dry-mouthed. I clutched my throat, looking over at Dallas. "Can I have some water?" I stood, took a wobbly step forward, and suddenly collapsed to the ground.

Everything went black.

Chapter Twenty-Four

Skye

I opened my eyes to find myself in a stark, white hospital room. The steady beeping of a heart monitor sounded from somewhere nearby. I moved my head to the right. Bright sun peeked around the edges of the window shades, forming vivid borders around two white squares.

I moved my head in the other direction, the muscles in my neck stiff and achy. Two blurry figures seated next to the bed came into focus. It was Teddy…and Caroline. Teddy slumped forward in a chair, his hands folded on his lap. Caroline leaned toward him, her whole body angled in his direction. Her lips hovered inches from his ear and moved with words I couldn't hear as her hand grasped his forearm.

Saliva filled my mouth and my heart jumped to frantic life. What was I witnessing? Were they…?

"T-Teddy?"

A barely audible squeak escaped my lips. Neither one of them heard me. I struggled to pull myself up.

Suddenly, it was as if Teddy's whole body was seized with electricity. His eyes bulged and his fingers grasped the arms of his chair.

"Skye?" His voice was a gasp.

He lurched across the room and brought his face

close to mine. "You're awake." Tears filled his eyes. He looked frantically over his shoulder and then back to me. "I'm going to get someone—a doctor or a nurse. *Someone*." He ran from the room.

"How long have I been asleep?" I asked, my voice coming out more like a croak.

"Two weeks." Caroline stood, her arms crossed and the edges of her lips turned downward. After a beat, she sauntered over, leaning so close to me I could smell her sour breath as she spoke.

"You're lucky to be alive. From what I hear, the bullet was really close to killing you."

She held my gaze for a few seconds until Teddy and two nurses burst into the room behind her.

"Welcome back, Miss Peters," one of them said as if we were old friends.

A thirty-something man breezed into the room. He had a strong jawline, thick hair that he continually flicked out of his eyes, and a white lab coat with a name tag reading "Dr. Jenkins".

"So glad to see you're awake." He leaned over me, touching some machines behind my bed. "How are you feeling?"

I considered his question. "Pretty good, overall…"

"No headache? Nausea?"

I shook my head.

"Wonderful. Maybe tonight we can see how you handle some solid food. Any special requests? I'm sure we can accommodate them."

I scrunched up my features, struggling to remember what I liked to eat.

"Do you know what happened to you, Skye?" Dr. Jenkins asked.

"A man broke into our hotel room. And shot me."

"That's right. You were shot in the chest. We conducted emergency surgery to remove the bullet and you've been in a coma since then—for two weeks. I believe you will recover and be back to normal again soon. Nothing short of a miracle, really."

I glanced down, taking in the ugly hospital gown and a mishmash of wires that were attached to my chest. I placed my hand a few inches beneath the nape of my neck and felt a thick bandage there.

Dr. Jenkins clasped his hands together. "I'll let you rest. I'll be back to check on you in a bit."

When Dr. Jenkins and the nurses had left, I turned my gaze to Teddy. "What happened? Who was it? Did they catch him?"

Teddy stepped up to the bed, his arms crossed over his stomach. "They think he was just trying to get some money. And, yeah, they caught him…he's in a coma. From the blow to the head I gave the bastard."

"Were you shot?"

"He grazed my leg."

"Thank God it was nothing more serious." I held out my hand to Teddy and he took it. Caroline lurked in the background.

Teddy looked away, avoiding my gaze. I knew I had been in a coma and all, but something about him was different. Distant. I barely noticed, though, amidst my excitement that Teddy was mine again. All mine.

Some time after, my parents and Maxie arrived. The atmosphere became joyful and boisterous.

"Thank God you're back," my mother said, wiping away tears.

She leaned forward to embrace me, then stared at

me for several minutes with a look of amazement.

"I had the weirdest experience when I was in the coma," I told Maxie once my mom, my dad, and Teddy were engaged in a conversation. Caroline had finally left.

"Oh yeah?" Maxie sat down on the edge of my bed. "What was it like?"

"It was like I was in another life." I kept my voice low, hoping my parents and Teddy couldn't hear. "But everything was so real. It wasn't like a normal dream."

"Well, no it wouldn't be. You were in a coma, sweetie. For *weeks*." She stroked my cheek.

I swallowed, unsatisfied with her answer. It didn't seem possible that what I'd just experienced had been a product of a coma. Yet it didn't seem possible for it to be anything else either.

"So what were you doing in this other life?" Maxie asked, a glow emanating from her cheeks.

I inhaled. "I was a pop star, a really famous one. I lived in a huge mansion in Bel Air with, like, twenty cars. And I was married."

"To Teddy?"

"No. To a record producer. A real person named Mark Campbell."

"You were married to someone else?" Teddy broke in.

I looked over to find my parents and him staring at me.

"In my dream, yes." I attempted a laugh, though it came out more like a croak.

Teddy's jaw clenched. I had been hiding from Teddy's proposal when I had been shot. Clearly he had not forgotten.

I needed to tell him everything had changed. Everything was different now. I knew I wanted to spend the rest of my life with him. I only hoped he still felt the same way. I hoped I wasn't too late.

Chapter Twenty-Five

Skye - Three Months Later

Sissy Stone and Mark Campbell were getting divorced. It had been the main focus at Pepperlake PR for the past two months. Francesca had already spun the story spectacularly for our client, using the opportunity to make Sissy Stone appear like a phoenix rising from the ashes—exactly what she had promised to do for me. The goal was to make Sissy seem even more sexy and appealing than before and yet somehow also more relatable…someone us average folk could truly understand.

Sissy continued to be unpleasant to deal with as always. But I saw her differently now. I knew her life was far from perfect, as was her self-esteem—even if I wasn't entirely sure I hadn't hallucinated the whole experience. Yet today our task did not require interacting with the prickly, self-adoring, endlessly vain pop star. It involved interacting with her soon-to-be ex. Mark. Someone I knew *intimately* well.

Three months after I emerged from my coma, the alternate life I had experienced continued to feel as lucid as ever. My time as a world-famous pop star was not like a dream that simply faded away. No, instead it was like a past that stayed with you forever. One that also made me feel crazy.

"I'd love to continue on as your PR professional," Francesca said from a dimly lit table across from Mark. "I can assure you I will be able to serve both you and your soon-to-be ex-wife equally well."

The Michelin-star restaurant, Flo, where Mark, Francesca, and I were currently dining was one I could never afford on my own. Not in this life anyway. Dark and moody with engraved panels and red velvet on the walls, the place was swarming with aging movie executives, young scantily-clad starlets, and hip celebrity couples. A live orchestra played jazz in the corner.

Mark dabbed the corners of his mouth with a napkin, his eyes intense as he stared at Francesca. "I appreciate that, but I think it's best if we part ways. Good to do business with you. Ladies." He rose from the table and nodded down at us gallantly, holding my gaze with his lips pulled up ever so slightly at the edges.

As he turned, I let my eyes wander over his frame. Tonight he was dressed in a three-piece suit that showed off his impressive shoulders and chest. His thick, dark beard only increased his sex appeal.

"So nice to see you." Francesca stood up and held out her hand. Mark gave her hand a quick shake and winked at me.

"Well, I'm off," Francesca said, once Mark had disappeared toward the back of the restaurant. She dropped her cell phone into her handbag and exhaled. "Mission accomplished. He signed the non-disclosure and Sissy is in the clear. That's all I wanted."

I forced a smile, sad for Sissy. I knew what it felt like to be in her position. Lonely was the only word that came to mind.

"Maybe you should stay awhile," Francesca said. "You *are* a single lady now." She lifted her eyebrows at me and disappeared toward the front door.

At the mention of "single," Teddy's face appeared in my vision and a brick formed in my stomach. Once I was home from the hospital and sufficiently healed, he had told me he needed space. *From me.* He was wounded from my less-than-receptive response to his proposal and nothing I said seemed to make it any better. I knew I was different, but it was too late to heal my relationship with Teddy—the man I now knew I wanted to spend the rest of my life with.

My parents had returned upstate earlier in the month and Maxie, who had temporarily moved in with me for three weeks, was currently spending the weekend holed up with her hot new boytoy. Maybe Francesca was right. Who did I have to get home to?

I meandered over to the bar and settled into one of the cushy, red-topped barstools. I was just lifting a glass of pink Chardonnay to my lips when a gravelly voice made me jump.

"Need any company?"

I looked sideways to find Mark removing his suit jacket. He placed it on a barstool on the far side and slid onto the stool next to mine. His crisp white button-down and dark gray vest only enhanced the bulging curves of his muscles. "Grey Goose Martini," he told the bartender before turning his attention back to me. "So you *do* drink?"

"Yes. I wasn't drinking before because Francesca prefers we not do so with clients…"

The bartender handed Mark his drink and he lifted

it to me. "Cheers."

"Cheers." I clanked my glass against his.

"So you're saying we're being naughty?"

I rolled my eyes, but smiled involuntarily.

"So, tell me, Skye—has public relations always been your dream job?"

I laugh-snorted. "No. I wanted to be a singer, actually. That's why I moved to LA."

He raised his eyebrows as he took in this new information. "I see. Made any progress in that arena?"

I swallowed nervously, then took another swig of my wine. "Well, I'm doing an open mic night next week for the first time." The thought of it made my stomach turn in a million somersaults. I did love singing and I didn't need a sea of adoring fans to do what I loved. I would just have to press on, regardless of the sheer terror I felt.

"Nice. You got guts."

I watched Mark as he took a slow sip of his Martini. He truly was a beautiful man. I knew I wasn't the only one who noticed either, because at least two women had checked him out in the last five minutes.

"So how are you doing with everything?" I asked.

Mark looked at me, surprised. "With the divorce? Eh, it's fine. Onward and upward."

"How are Comet and Lucienne?"

Mark placed his drink down on the bar and fixed his gaze on me. "You know my kids?"

I swallowed. "N-no, I don't know them…more know *of* them, I guess."

This seemed to satisfy him. He relaxed his posture and turned back toward the bar. "Ah. They're good. Staying with my ex-wife—my first ex-wife, their mother—while I find a new place to live. Sissy got the house, as you know. They're not a fan of my bachelor pad."

I thought of his children—my former stepchildren—the ones I knew so well. My heart ached to see them. I realized I missed them.

Crap. I really needed to see a therapist.

"What about you, Freckles? Anybody special in your life?"

My heart rammed against the inside of my ribcage. *Freckles*? Did he really just call me his nickname for me from the other life? From when I was his wife?

"Why'd you call me that?"

He lifted one side of his mouth into a half-smile and stared at me for a beat before lightly running a finger over the bridge of my nose. "Because of these. What? No one's ever called you that before?"

"Oh…yes, *somebody* has…"

He turned away and swirled his drink as he stared into it. "Damn. I wasn't the first."

"No…and there is nobody special. My boyfriend and I broke up recently."

Mark placed one of his large hands on my thigh and pressed his fingers into the tender flesh there. "Wanna get out of here?"

I stared down at his hand as he stared at me. Mark and his Scottish accent were clearly hot, and going home with him was undeniably tempting. I was fully single after all. Yet I knew exactly where a relationship with him would lead. The best I could hope for was to be ex-wife number three. Mark was simply not a one-woman man—and there was nothing sexy about that.

"Skye?"

My heartbeat abruptly increased at the familiar voice filling my consciousness. I twisted my neck to find Teddy standing a foot away.

"What are you doing here?" I asked.

"Can I talk to you?"

Mark removed his hand from my thigh as I slid off the bench. I trailed Teddy into a nearby corner.

"How'd you know where I was?" I asked.

Teddy glared over my shoulder toward the bar. Toward Mark.

"The Find My Friends app? You still have yours enabled."

"Okay…"

"And you weren't answering your phone. I needed to see you." He locked eyes with me. "They arrested Caroline. She was behind everything. She hired the man who broke into the hotel room. The one who tried to kill you. The *psychopath*."

My heart dropped to my feet. That made a lot of sense and yet…*kill me?* "Wait, how do the police know all this? And why did Caroline want to kill me?" A chill crawled up my spine, a recognition of how close I was to dying.

"The man she hired? The one I bludgeoned? He woke up and started talking. As to why…" Teddy's cheeks reddened as he stared at the floor. "They seem to think Caroline had some kind of obsession with me. That she wanted to get you out of the way or something…"

"Well, *did* she have an obsession with you?"

Teddy released a slow breath as he looked up at me. "She was upset when I told her I was going to ask you to marry me. I know that much."

"Wow."

"Well, she's in jail now. And I'm going to do everything in my power to make sure she stays there a long time." Teddy's eyes wandered back over to the bar. "Who's he?"

I glanced over my shoulder, momentarily forgetting about Mark. "He's a client." *And my ex-husband.*

Teddy clenched his jaw and jammed his hands into his pockets. "I miss you, Skye."

A flame flickered in my chest. "You do?"

"Of course I do." He reached out and took my hand, the feel of his bare skin against mine sending electricity from my head to my toes.

"Does that mean you believe me now? That something changed while I was in that coma? I realized I don't want to live without you."

Teddy's eyes softened as he continued to grasp my hand. "Yes. I believe you. Can I call you tomorrow?"

I bit my lip, breaking out into a smile. "Yes."

He nodded at me, his eyes sparkling, before heading toward the exit.

"That the ex?" Mark said when I returned to the bar.

"Yes." I lifted my purse from the floor. "I better go home. It was nice chatting."

Mark smiled. As I stared into his eyes, I could almost see the past we shared together. Maybe some part of him felt our history, too.

Mark took a final swig of his martini, set it down on the bar, and stood.

"Call my assistant and tell her where you're singing next week. I'll send one of my people out to check you out. Who knows—you could be the next big thing." Mark handed me a business card. I stared down at it.

"Really?"

He lifted his suit jacket from the barstool, tossed it over his shoulder, and strolled away. "Good talking to you too, Freckles. See you around."

A feeling of hope took flight in my chest. I slid Mark's card into a side pocket of my bag, then blindly dug around in its contents for my keys. My fingers happened upon something smooth and slender—a shape I didn't recognize. I pulled the item from the depths of my bag. It was a solid gold bangle. Not my own. Had it slipped off Francesca's wrist and fallen into my bag somehow?

Just as I was about to slide it back into my bag, something on the inside of the bracelet caught my eye. An engraved message. I brought it close to my face and struggled to read it in the dark restaurant. "To my sun, my moon…my Skye. Love, Mark."

A mixture of shock and calm overtook me. I placed the bracelet carefully into a zipper pouch of my bag.

I already knew the truth. Still it was good to have something physical from my experience to prove what I felt inside. This would be my reminder.

Chapter Twenty-Six

Caroline - A year-and-a-half later

I sat in the familiar, mahogany-rich office of Dr. Threnbow, staring out as the bright sun filtered through the swaying leaves of the trees outside. This office was a place I'd been in countless times over the past year. Ever since my conviction and subsequent seven-year sentence.

Convicting me for being in love…idiots.

"Sorry I'm late, Caroline."

I shifted in the leather chair as my psychiatrist took a seat across from me. He pulled a notebook and a pen from his pocket and crossed a brown leather loafer over his knee.

"How are you feeling now that the weekend has passed? Now that Teddy and Skye are married?"

I inhaled and turned my gaze back to the sunny day once again. *This again? Booorrring.*

"I'm feeling fine, actually. Ted is firmly in my rearview. Someone so deluded as to mess up his life by marrying that moron, Skye, isn't worth my time." I shrugged, meeting Dr. Threnbow's gaze. "I tried to warn him. So I'm fine."

The doctor furrowed his brow and pursed his lips at me, before scribbling something messily on his pad. "I see. It sounds as if you're still harboring some feelings for Ted. Am I correct?"

"And?"

"And it doesn't make Ted a bad or a stupid person because he married someone you do not like. Do you feel strong enough to try what we discussed last week?"

I felt no reaction to the thought of what he was proposing. "Why not?"

Dr. Threnbow reached into his shirt pocket, pulled out a folded piece of paper, and handed it to me. I unfolded the paper. It was a black-and-white printout of an image. Skye was being spun on the dance floor by Ted. She was smiling widely in a white sleeveless bridal gown as he, dashing, of course, and dressed in a tux, stared at his new bride adoringly.

I glanced up. "I'm fine."

"I'm glad to hear that, Caroline. I believe you've made significant progress since we started meeting." Dr. Threnbow cocked his head and brought the pen to his mouth. "Still, I wonder if you shouldn't refrain from searching his name again in the future. To prevent additional distress."

"But I want to know when he gets divorced, of course." I smiled.

Dr. Threnbow grimaced. "I can't tell if you're joking, Caroline. But if you're not, I want to assert that I believe that is a very unhealthy thing to hope for. Even if Ted *did* get divorced, he knows you hired someone to kill Skye. He would likely never consider you a suitable life partner. Wouldn't you agree?"

"I was joking, Doctor. I no longer desire Ted. His decision to wed Skye fully cured me of any attraction to him." I put my palms up in the air as if to present myself. "See? All healed. Can I be released now?"

"I don't agree you're all healed. But I do believe you're a lovely, highly intelligent woman who can live a full and satisfying life once you are released."

Dr. Threnbow's words caused something to flutter in my chest. As I locked eyes with the doctor, I noticed their striking chestnut hue. And his shoulders. Even though he had a decade on me, he was strong and well-built. How had I never noticed him before?

I glanced down at my prison-issued T-shirt and cargo pants and fingered my hair, suddenly aware of my appearance. Next week I would wear lipstick and eyeliner. I would make my hair presentable and slather my skin with scented lotion.

My gaze wandered to two photos on Dr. Threnbow's desk. I had noticed them before, but never studied them. One showed a middle-aged woman standing in the woods alongside two teenage children, a girl and a boy. The woman's blonde hair was graying. The other photo was of the doctor and the woman posing in formalwear. They were frozen in laughter and grasping glasses of champagne.

So that was his wife.

I glanced back at Dr. Threnbow. He could do better than her. In fact, he and I would look infinitely better as a couple.

I felt something growing within me, something coming alive. It all made sense now. Everything. I had only cared for Ted so I would eventually find my way here. To Dr. Threnbow.

He was my destiny.

"Do you agree? That you are capable of finding someone once you are released?" he asked.

The corner of my mouth twitched into a smile.

"Yes. Maybe even before."

Dr. Threnbow smiled. It was the most beautiful thing I had ever set eyes on.

"I'm happy to hear that. There is someone out there who is an even better match for you than you believe Ted is."

Ted who?

Chapter Twenty-Seven

Skye - Three weeks later

"This is the seat we have reserved for you." The hostess of Tempting Thai held out her hand toward a table on a raised podium. It had a view of the busy street through a bay window on one side and the restaurant on the other.

"Actually…is there somewhere more private?" I asked.

Teddy's hand rested in the small of my back. "Really?"

"Yes." I smiled at him.

The hostess led us farther into the restaurant and directed us to a high back booth with warm overhead lighting and candles. We both slid into the same side. Newlyweds.

It had been a month since Teddy and I had wed. It felt both surreal and perfectly natural. That's how I knew it was right.

"You sounded amazing tonight." Teddy grinned at me.

Since trying out open mic night over a year earlier, I had become a fixture at several local restaurants. I'd established a few solid professional relationships with restaurant owners and had even witnessed people coming to see me multiple times. No autograph signing—yet.

Mark's team had reached out to say they thought I had potential but wanted me to get a little more experience. Possibilities were on the horizon. Excitement was bubbling.

"I have something to ask you," Teddy said.

I glanced down at the ring on my finger, the diamond dancing in the candlelight. A few weeks after we started dating again, I started dropping hints that Teddy should propose. The answer would be different this time, I assured him. Luckily, he caught on quickly and popped the question.

I sometimes wondered about his wife in the previous life. If she existed somewhere. If maybe he even knew her. I felt a certain kinship with her—we did love the same man, after all.

"What would you think about doing a duet together on the show?"

I broke out into a smile. "I'd love that."

Teddy wrapped his arm around me and pulled me close.

"How is it we've never done a duet before?" He lowered his mouth to my shoulder and kissed it.

"It's amazing, isn't it?"

I pictured the day I'd visited his show. The little girl who'd outed me, the reverence the audience had shown me when they realized who I was. *The* Skye Peters.

Did I feel a pang at the loss of those millions of fans? Their adoration was genuine after all, real enough to warm up my center for awhile.

No. I had zero regrets. I would trade it away every time for my so-called average existence. My perpetual sense of dissatisfaction had vanished. I sunk into the deliciousness of each supposedly mundane moment with an overwhelming sense of appreciation.

I had no idea that true happiness could be so subtle that no one outside of the few people experiencing it could understand it. I thought things had to be shared to mean something. But all sharing everything means is you're living through others. Once I got that, people's opinions stopped mattering so much to me.

After the waitress dropped off our meals—Teddy's was a garlic-drenched crispy shrimp plate and mine was salmon and vegetables in sweet curry—Teddy sat back.

"Photo?" he said.

"You know I don't do that anymore. My social media accounts have been deleted. I'm so much happier for it too."

Teddy smiled and dug into his meal. I watched him eat, then picked up my fork and sliced off a piece of saucy salmon.

Teddy glanced at me from the side of his eyes.

"What?" I asked.

"Do you ever think about her? About Caroline?"

"Of course. It's the stuff of nightmares. She tried to have me killed. It's changed me forever." I set my fork down on my plate and wiped the corners of my mouth with a paper napkin. "But I'm okay."

Teddy grimaced and rubbed his hands across his face. His brown eyes met mine, their depths taking my breath away. "I'm so sorry."

"I know you are. We got through it. We'll keep getting through it." I took Teddy's hand under the table, the way our fingers interlaced sparking something deep in my stomach. "I love you."

He leaned forward and kissed me, and the way his lips massaged mine transported me out of the restaurant for a moment. When he leaned back against the booth, his cheeks were flushed.

"If she ever tries anything again…" Hatred spread across Teddy's features. It was a side he rarely showed.

"Shhh." I stroked his cheek.

Our meals gone, I rested my head on Teddy's shoulder.

"I have something to ask you too," I said.

Teddy—my husband—lifted an eyebrow. "Yes, Mrs. Peters-Sorens?"

"What would you think about…expanding our family?"

Teddy's face went slack. He looked away, searching the restaurant.

Shoot. We'd only been married a month. What was I doing? Why was I in a rush?

Teddy brought his gaze back to mine. "I think…let's start tonight."

We went home that night to begin our average, miraculous adventure. And we shared our plan with exactly no one.

Real Love
by Ted Sorens

The highest mountain top, the deepest creek,
If I lost my hearing and I couldn't speak.
Halfway around the world and all the way too,
There's nothing—and no one—that could keep me
away from you

The itchiest poison ivy, the scratchiest sore throat.
Even if you lived in a stone castle with a moat.
I'd find a way through and I'd keep going til I knew
I could reach out my arms and wrap them tightly
around you

Because when you're not with me, the sun abruptly
goes
The birds stop their singing and the rivers cease to flow.
At least that's how it seems and that's how I feel
I guess that's how you know your love is real

Blonde Me
By Billie Bird

Ex-girl ain't no ex at all
She picks up the phone whenever I call
Says she'll make room for me when I'm comin' through
Don't kid yourself, Old Man, she ain't true to you

I've got what it takes and I don't make mistakes
When I get her started, she never hits the brakes
If she told you what you got keeps her satisfied
I got news for you, Old News: your girl lied

Stop playin' the fool, she's playin' with me
Your daydream is over and your bed is empty
You had your moment and you couldn't keep up
Sayonara Grandpa I got your chick locked up

A word about the author…

Pamela grew up in Springfield, Missouri, where she often escaped into her own imagination as Alice in Wonderland, making up stories in this imaginary world. She wrote her first novel with scented markers in the first grade. Since then, she's penned many poems, short stories, and a few novels. Pamela's stories often include characters being thrown into unfamiliar worlds, likely inspired by some of her favorite movies from childhood.

In addition to writing fiction, Pamela is an experienced copywriter and journalist. She has a Bachelor's degree in Psychology and Creative Writing from Missouri State University and a Masters from the University of Missouri School of Journalism. Pamela's non-fiction has been featured in a variety of magazines and her short fiction has received an honorable mention in the Women on Writing Flash Fiction Contest.

Pamela lives in the Kansas City area with her husband and two young children. For a free bonus story about Skye, visit https://pamelamahajan.com

Thank you for purchasing
this publication of The Wild Rose Press, Inc.

For questions or more information
contact us at
info@thewildrosepress.com.

The Wild Rose Press, Inc.
www.thewildrosepress.com